THE KING OF SLIPPERY FALLS

SID HITE

SCHOLASTIC PRESS

NEW YORK

FOR ALL THE GOOD PEOPLE FROM VEJER WHO FED AND ENTERTAINED ME DURING MY STAY IN THEIR VILLAGE. — S. H.

LIBRARY OF CONGRESS CATALOGING-IN-PUBLICATION DATA • Hite, Sid.
The King of Slippery Falls / by Sid Hite.
1st ed.   p. cm. • Summary: While on a single-minded quest to catch an elusive giant trout, sixteen-year-old Lewis Hinton's life in a small Idaho town is turned upside down when he learns that he is adopted and might be a descendant of French royalty. [1. Identity — Fiction. 2. Adoption — Fiction. 3. Fishing — Fiction. 4. France — History — 17th century — Fiction. 5. Idaho — Fiction.] I. Title.
ISBN : 0 - 4 3 9 - 3 4 2 5 7 - 0
PZ7.H62964Ki 2004 [Fic] — dc21
2002091212 • 10 9 8 7 6
5 4 3 2 1   04 05
06 07 08

Printed in the U.S.A. 23 • First edition, May 2004 • The display type was set in P22 Daddy-O-Square. The text type was set in JoannaMT. Illustration © 2004 by Dan Yaccarino. Book design by Marijka Kostiw

APPARENTLY

THERE IS NOTHING

THAT CANNOT HAPPEN.

— MARK TWAIN

THE STATE OF

IDAHO EXISTS,

AND MAPS OF

THAT STATE

INDICATE THE

PRESENCE OF A

RIVER CALLED

THE LITTLE LOST.

OTHERWISE,

THE SETTING

FOR THIS STORY

IS PURE FICTION.

SO ARE THE

CHARACTERS,

I THINK.

ONE

Lewis Hinton hurried home from Slippery Falls High, deposited his books on a table in the hallway, grabbed his fishing gear from the garage, and headed toward Slippery Falls Park. The four-acre preserve was less than a mile from his house. It was situated on the east side of the small, Idaho town where he lived, which was also called Slippery Falls. The name was taken from a thunderous waterfall that plummeted into a rocky gorge below the park. It, too, was called Slippery Falls. Only the high-plain river that fed the falls had a different name. It was known as the Little Lost.

The date was Friday, May the fourth, early in the twenty-first century. The sun was bright in a cloudless, blue sky, and the Rocky Mountain air was fresh with spring. Finally, winter had loosened its gelid grip over southern Idaho, and the inhabitants of Slippery Falls were stepping happily outdoors again.

The fishing gear Lewis had grabbed from the garage was unique for the region in which he lived. Indeed, his thirteen-foot-long rod was roughly twice the length of an ordinary, freshwater pole. It was a custom job, designed specifically for fishing from an elevated jag of rock on the west side of the steep cliffs by the park. Lewis was the only person in town who fished from the cliffs. No one else dared the risky climb.

Lewis knew his fishing pole was viewed as an amusing peculiarity by the town's older, supposedly wiser, fishermen. He knew because the men mocked him openly. They did not deride him meanly, yet were consistent, and Lewis frequently heard remarks such as, "Hey, the ocean is that way," or, "You aiming to vault across the gorge with that tree?" or, "I don't believe the whales are biting today."

Lewis did his best to ignore the teasing. *Let the codgers have their fun,* he thought. One day he'd walk by them with the biggest fish ever hauled out of the Little Lost and watch them swallow their tongues.

Lewis was three blocks north of the park when he saw Maple Baderhoovenlisterah kneeling by a flower bed in her front yard. A model of hope for anyone fearing the ravages of age, the eighty-eight-year-old Maple was inordinately vibrant and spry, and did not look a day over seventy. She behaved even younger. Maple was what is called one of a kind.

She was attired today in a homemade, blue-and-green-checkered dress that fell to her ankles. She owned at least a dozen outfits meeting this description, with one varying only slightly from the others in shades of color or the size of the squares constituting the check pattern. Lewis once asked why she owned so many similar dresses, and she answered with a knowing grin, "Because I was wearing a blue-and-green dress when I met my husband and I figure they're the fashion for me."

Lewis stopped at the gate and said politely, "How do you do, Mrs. Baderhoovenlisterah?"

She looked up and smiled. "I do splendidly, Lewis. How about yourself?"

Lewis shrugged and said he was okay. Both he and Maple knew he was confused about his identity. They'd discussed the matter on several occasions during the past year. It was that year that had seen them go from casual acquaintances to intimate friends. Sympathy was the catalyst that drew them together, for the previous May they had both suffered a crisis in their personal lives. First, Lewis had discovered the shocking news that he was adopted, then a few days later Maple's husband, Wickham Baderhoovenlisterah, died after a bad bout of bookworms.

Maple nodded at Lewis's fishing pole and said, "Going after the big one again, I see. That's good, Lewis. Luck often sides with persistence."

Lewis smiled thinly. "I hope it sides with me today."

"Me, too."

"Thanks. So, guess I'll be going now."

Maple bobbed her head, raised her garden trowel, and pointed it at Lewis. "Should you stumble across a patch of free time in the next week or so, why don't you pop by and pay me a proper visit."

"I will," Lewis replied sincerely. Visiting Maple was never a chore.

Lewis crossed through Slippery Falls Park and halted at a six-foot-high iron fence protecting pedestrians from a precipitous, two-hundred-foot drop into the river gorge below. Lewis passed his rod through the fence, removed his shoes and socks, scaled the barrier, and dropped down onto a narrow ledge of rock. The ledge was broken in places, irregular of plane and suspended high over a line of jagged boulders hugging the riverbank below.

Any normal person in such a position would have trembled with fright. Not Lewis. He grabbed his rod and started across the near-vertical cliff face with the surefooted confidence of a goat.

Lewis's relaxed manner on the cliff was in stark contrast with his typical mental state since learning he was not the natural progeny of his parents, Martha and Avery Hinton.

According to the story he had been told, Avery was walking on Hidden Lane when an unfamiliar woman stepped from behind a tree and placed a basket before him. Obviously distressed and speaking in heavily accented English, the woman told Avery, "He Lewis, my boy. Please, mister, for you to keep care." Avery had stared wide-eyed at the woman, then bent to peer in the basket. When he looked up, the woman had withdrawn into the surrounding forest and disappeared.

Avery carried the basket home to Martha, who took one look at the child swaddled within and fell in love. Later that evening, while removing soiled blankets from the basket, Martha found a sealed envelope. Printed on the envelope were the words: GIVE WHEN LITTLE MAN.

The envelope and presumed letter within disturbed Martha. Having already decided that Lewis was hers to keep, she spent the next two years anguishing over the missive before mentioning it to Avery. She did so casually one evening at dinner. "Sweetheart, how old were you when you started shaving?"

"Sixteen or thereabouts," Avery replied. "Why do you ask?"

"Oh . . . well, because there was a letter for Lewis in the basket he came home in. It says, 'Give when little man.'" Martha ignored the incredulous look on her husband's face, ate a brussels sprout, and continued: "We will tell Lewis he was adopted on his fifteenth birthday. I'll give him the letter when he turns sixteen."

Avery had gazed at his wife for a long while without voicing any of the questions passing through his mind. He loved and trusted Martha, and accepted that the matter had been judiciously decided.

Lewis completed his daring scramble across the cliff and settled on his regular sitting rock high above the Little Lost River gorge. As far as he knew, he was the only person ever to sit upon this particular stone. It was his personal rock — his private retreat from the anxiety-filled world on the far side of the fence. He'd discovered it the previous May, the day after his fifteenth birthday. Despair had driven him out onto the cliffs, and instinct had guided him toward the upper lip of river. By chance, he reached and climbed onto the rock just as wind gusted through the gorge and parted the frothy curtain of Slippery Falls. In that instant, he saw a pool of water that had heretofore been concealed behind the falls. Within the pool he saw (or thought he saw) the shadow of a huge fish. It was just a glimpse — for the wind quickly died and closed the curtain — yet the sighting lifted his downcast spirits and inspired him with a purpose. "I'm going to catch that fish," he determined with a resolve that did not wane between then and now, despite repeated failed attempts.

Indeed, in the year since sighting the aquatic monster and building his custom rod, Lewis had caught nary a minnow. That was fine with him. If merely catching a fish was all he wished to accomplish, he would've dropped a line from the bridge south of town where the regular crowd routinely pulled in perch, pickerel, and gar. Lewis, however, was not interested in small fry. He wanted the big one, which time and his imagination had transformed into a gigantic rainbow trout more than forty inches long.

He inspected the lead on his lure (a silver spoon with a red-feathered tail), drew his rod over a shoulder, and whipped it around. Line zinged from the reel. The lure plunged through the cascading wall of water and into the pool behind the falls. Or so Lewis hoped, just as he also hoped a backwash current swirled his bait seductively about.

Lewis watched his line and waited, his senses soothed by the sonorous song of the falling Little Lost. The springtime sun fell like a blessing on his pale, winter face.

Time passed.

Patience is the virtue of all good fishermen. It is both a task and a reward.

More time ticked by.

Soon the sun dipped below the western mountain peaks and flooded the canyon below Lewis's feet with shadows. He waited a brief while longer for the giant trout to strike, then reluctantly reeled in his line and retraced his path along the cliff face.

He had half-hoisted himself onto the ledge by the fence when he was startled by a voice and nearly fell backward.

"I knew you were there," the voice trilled triumphantly. "Your shoes gave you away."

Lewis caught himself and continued upward, and soon stood face-to-face with Amanda Dot. If not for the fence between them, they were close enough for kissing — an appealing notion for Lewis, yet something he'd never brought himself to try. "What's to give away?" he asked, sticking his fishing gear through the fence and beginning to climb. "I wasn't hiding."

"Perhaps not," Amanda retorted, "but if you were hiding, I would've found you."

"No doubt," Lewis allowed after landing on the park side of the fence and sitting by his shoes.

Amanda squatted so that she was eye to eye with Lewis. "I was thinking about your problem and I figured out what you should do."

Lewis grimaced. His chest grew tight, and he had difficulty breathing. "What did you figure?"

Amanda pushed an errant lock of brown hair from her pretty, round face. "It's simple, really. Don't know why I never thought of it before."

"What?"

"Write a letter or send an e-mail to the National Archives in Washington, D.C. They must have some record of who you are."

Lewis concentrated on tying the laces of his shoes. When he was done, he stood and inquired sarcastically, "What do you suggest I tell the people in Washington? That I was found in a basket? That some woman with a foreign accent stepped from behind a tree and foisted me upon my father?"

Although Amanda did not approve of

Lewis's tone, she could hear the pain in his voice and excused his scornful manner. She hooked arms with him and started walking, and waited until they were halfway across the park before saying, "You know, Lewis, you have a choice. You can feel sorry for yourself from now until kingdom come, or you can accept the facts and be happy."

"I wish it was that easy."

Amanda let five seconds pass. "Choosing happiness is as hard or easy as you make it."

Lewis's chest grew tighter. Amanda had a point, of course. She usually did. Still . . . he couldn't quite find his happiness switch.

TWO

Before parting in the park and going to their respective homes for dinner, Amanda and Lewis made plans to rendezvous that evening at Chip's Coffee Shop in downtown Slippery Falls. The restaurant was easy to find, as the town's commercial district was only two blocks long, putting downtown about three feet west of uptown. The mayor, Constance Greenly, who owned and operated a variety store on Main Street, was forever trying to attract new businesses and tourists to Slippery Falls, but for reasons beyond her control, the town refused to grow. Even so, Constance was not an easily deterred woman and continued to dream of Slippery Falls as a premiere leisure destination in northwest America. For the time being, there was Chip's: the one and only hangout for teenagers desiring the hint of a social life in town.

Amanda and Lewis were ensconced in their

preferred booth in the front window by eight-fifteen, waiting for Speedy Montana to deliver the milk shakes they had ordered. Experience had taught them not to expect their beverages soon. Speedy was forgetful, easily distracted, and slower than an arthritic turtle.

Amanda gave Lewis an earful while they waited. "Listen, Mister Too-Blue-for-Comfort, if you don't want my help, just say so. You're not the only one with problems around here."

"I'm not?"

"Of course not. There are plenty of people I could be helping."

"Like who?" Lewis was genuinely curious.

"Well, me for example," Amanda answered tersely. "I could be helping me."

Lewis hemmed. "And what exactly is your problem?"

"Must I spell it out?"

"If you want me to know, yes."

Amanda huffed. "For starters, I'm too kindhearted. It's a compulsion I must learn to control if I'm ever going to make it as a recording artist. They're expected to be surly, you know. Not sweet to everybody like me."

"I see," said Lewis. He wanted to believe Amanda had enough talent to prosper in the music business, yet since she refused to sing in public or in private for his benefit, he was unable to judge her chances of success. As for the sweetness of her nature — it varied. "So . . . any other problems I should know about, Amanda?"

"My nose is covered with freckles."

"You have a cute nose."

Amanda rolled her big, dark eyes. "If I wanted cute, I'd buy a Chihuahua. A woman's nose should be pretty."

Lewis grinned. Conversing with Amanda was almost enough to make him forget his anxieties.

"Let's not talk about me. You're the emotional wreck at this table. Now do you or don't you want help figuring out who you are?"

Lewis replied brusquely, "Let's keep some perspective here. I may be confused about who I am and where I came from, but that doesn't make me an emotional wreck."

"Fine. You're confused. I'm offering you my help."

"I appreciate the offer, but this is something I need to figure out alone."

"Why alone?"

Lewis hesitated. Amanda had asked a good question and, as a friend, deserved a fair answer. "It's hard to put into words, but I'll try to explain. The back of my hands, I know. My face, I've seen it thousands of times in the mirror. If I —"

"Such a handsome face, too," Amanda interjected. "Goes so nicely with your hair."

Lewis blushed. It was true, he had a fine-featured face with winsome, grayish blue eyes — topped off with enviably thick, golden brown curls — however, the quality of his looks had nothing to do with what he was saying before Amanda interrupted. "Never mind," he said. "I thought we were being serious."

"Sorry. Go ahead. I'm listening."

Lewis sighed and continued. "As I was about to say, I know myself outwardly, and my memories are mine — it's not as if I had a brain transplant or anything . . . but deep down in here" — Lewis jabbed his chest with a thumb — "there's been a hollow place ever since I learned I wasn't who I grew up thinking I was. Something that's supposed to be there is missing. Does that make sense?"

"Yes and no," Amanda equivocated. "I mean, I understand everything but the part about you not being who you grew up thinking you were."

Lewis tried another line of logic. "Try thinking of it this way. You're a Dot, you come from a long line of Dots, at least on your father's side, so you know your past. That's information I no longer have. For me . . . well, the whole ball of wax melted last year when I found out I was adopted."

"I see what you're saying now," Amanda allowed. "The Dots go way back to Texas, and before that, Missouri. All the males are boring — only female Dots have any pizzazz. My mom, by the way, was a Pullen from Minnesota. One out of every three Pullens is mentally unstable. Fortunately, I was spared the curse."

"I'm glad you were spared," said Lewis. "And you make my point for me. Your ancestors give you knowledge of yourself."

Amanda shrugged and turned toward the doorway as Gaston Fullup sauntered into Chip's. Gaston was sixteen, tall and dark-haired, and the closest thing the town had to a rich kid. His father was the owner and president of the Slippery Falls Footstool and Ladder Factory, the principal source of employment in the area and the company where Avery Hinton worked. Although Gaston was not arrogant and made no conscious effort to be different from others, he drove a red moped, subscribed to more than a dozen magazines, was a trendy dresser, and could not have blended into the background if he tried.

Amanda welcomed Gaston with a warm smile. Lewis took a deep breath and exhaled. Gaston bowed and offered, "Good evening, people. You're looking lovely as usual, Amanda."

Amanda slid toward the wall and patted the booth beside her. Gaston sat and asked Lewis, "What's happening?"

Lewis shrugged. He didn't dislike Gaston, but neither did he like him very much. The guy had an annoying knack for showing up every time Lewis and Amanda had a few minutes alone together. Worse, Amanda always seemed pleased when he appeared.

Gaston tried again to get a rise out of Lewis. "Any luck with that whopper you're trying to catch?"

"No."

"Oh. Well, hang in there, Lewis. Big dreams take time."

Lewis said nothing. The last thing he needed in his life was unsolicited, philosophical advice from Gaston. Amanda shot Lewis a look and was about to harangue him for being rude when Speedy Montana shuffled forward with two deluxe vanilla milk shakes.

"I'll have one of those," Gaston said to Speedy as she plopped the shakes on the table. He then informed Amanda and Lewis, "The shakes are on me."

"Thanks for treating, Gaston," Amanda cooed before applying her lips to the straw.

"You don't have to pay for me," said Lewis.

"I know that," replied Gaston. "But I want to, all right?"

"Fine," Lewis allowed. "If you insist."

Moments later, the door to Chip's swung open again and the remaining members of the clique that orbited around Amanda appeared. Their names were Misty Dean, Lob Borroughs, and Sophie Joilet. They were a diverse lot. The main thing they all had in common was living in Slippery Falls.

"Hello"s and "What's up?"s were exchanged, then Lewis slid from the booth and motioned for the trio to take his seat.

"You have a hot date?" asked Lob, sliding into the booth ahead of Misty and Sophie. Lob was a skinny, self-proclaimed antidisestablishmentarian with wire-rim glasses and a ponytail.

"No date," said Lewis.

"Where ya going, then?" wondered Misty. As usual, she was wearing one of the many hats from her extensive collection.

Lewis shrugged. "Nowhere, really."

"Not to nitpick or anything," said Gaston, "but I believe it's physically impossible to go nowhere."

"That's true," adjoined Amanda. "Although

spiritually, they say, nowhere is a very popular destination."

Lewis waited until the chuckling subsided. "It's nothing personal. I'm in the mood for a walk. That's all."

Amanda furrowed her brow at Lewis. "Right. You're walking straight to the park to dream about that fish no one has ever seen but you."

"The dream fish." Misty giggled.

"Yeah, Lewis," said Lob. "What's with you and that fish?"

Lewis shrugged. How could he explain what he didn't fully understand himself? "I don't know, Lob. Haven't you ever wanted something that you couldn't get off your mind until you had it?"

"Sure, but not for a whole year, and definitely not a fish."

"Each to their own," Gaston remarked with a grin.

"Enjoy your walk, Lewis," Sophie offered

sympathetically. She was pretty and petite, with a short bob haircut. Sophie was thought shy by people who didn't know her well. She wasn't. She was just reserved and difficult to read.

Lewis nodded to Sophie, then turned and departed. As he went through the door, Amanda hemmed and mused aloud, "I'm worried about Lewis. I hope he finds himself soon."

THREE

Lewis popped out of bed on Saturday morning and peered out the window. There was not a cloud in the sky. *Yes,* he thought. *The monster is mine today.*

After a quick breakfast, Lewis found Martha and Avery sitting on the back patio. "Morning, son," they greeted him almost simultaneously.

"Morning, Mom. Morning, Dad. I'm off for the day. See you later."

"What have you got planned?" Martha asked, then added before Lewis could reply, "Oh, never mind. I'm sure you're headed onto those perilous cliffs where one wrong move could break a mother's heart."

Lewis never knew how to respond when maternal pessimism got the best of Martha. He looked to Avery for assistance, but the man took a sip of coffee and left Lewis to his own defense. Lewis used reason. "Mom, would you rather me go riding in a car? There are hundreds of automobile accidents every day in this country. Being a passenger in a car is statistically more dangerous than rock climbing."

"Who said anything about statistics?" countered Martha.

"I just did, Mom. I was making a logical point."

Martha was not impressed. "Arguing numbers will get you nowhere with me. It's unsafe to climb on those cliffs. That's why no one but you goes out there."

Lewis hesitated. What could he say? As anyone who has ever had a mother knows, they are a worrisome lot who fret about whatever they choose, whenever they wish, for whatever reason. Avery had once tried to explain the distressed-mother phenomenon to Lewis. "There's a voice in the sky that only mothers hear. When it instructs them to worry, they worry. They have no recourse." At the time,

Lewis inquired what the voice sounded like, but Avery didn't know. Not being a mother, it had never spoken to him.

Back on the patio, Avery cleared his throat and said to Martha, "Let's not bury the wounded before the battle starts. Lewis has been climbing on those cliffs for a solid year and he hasn't fallen off yet."

Martha speared Avery with a pointed look.

"Well, he hasn't," Avery ventured sheepishly.

Lewis recognized an exit cue when he saw one. "I'll be home in time for dinner. I'll probably have lunch with Mrs. Baderhoovenlisterah. She invited me to stop by."

"Oh. And how is Maple?" wondered Avery.

"Fine, I think," said Lewis.

"Maple Baderhoovenlisterah is always fine," Martha said. "It's encoded in her nature."

Fishing is older than the Bible. Humans have been trying to catch fish since they climbed out of the trees. (Humans out, not the fish.) It is a chance activity. Sometimes you sit all day and catch a sunburn, or a mosquito in your mouth. Sometimes you drive a hook into your hand. Sometimes you get a nibble.

Lewis watched and waited and prayed for the big trout to strike his lure from quarter to nine until noon that Saturday. As usual, nothing happened. "You can only stay hidden so long. I'll get you," Lewis promised the trout before reeling in his line and starting back across the cliffs.

Maple Baderhoovenlisterah was standing in her front doorway when Lewis arrived. She seemed to have been expecting him. "There you are. Inclined for a little lunch, I suspect."

"Yes, ma'am." Lewis stepped through the gate and carefully laid his fishing pole beside a flower bed.

The foyer to Maple's house reeked with a stale, cheesy aroma. The odor emanated from a large, oval room on the right. It had originally been a living room, but was now occupied by rows of shelves stacked high with books. It was from these books that the inky bouquet of knowledge emerged.

Maple owned so many books that when the Slippery Falls Town Council was forced to shut the public library because of funding shortfalls, Mayor Greenly decreed that any citizen wishing to read should go to Maple's house and politely ask to borrow a book. Fortunately for all, Maple condoned the decree. There was, however, a twist that the reading public soon discovered: If you damaged or were delinquent returning one of Maple's books, you were apt to meet with some sort of bizarre accident, usually of a socially embarrassing nature. No one was maimed or killed in one of the mishaps — nor was there ever any proof that Maple was involved — yet the message was clear: If Maple lent you a book, you'd better take good care of the thing and return it when you said you would.

As Lewis followed Maple into the kitchen,

the smell of musty words yielded to baked apples, cinnamon, and mint. They sat at a table overlooking a rose garden and ate a macaroni casserole served warm from the oven. They knew each other well enough to converse and eat simultaneously. "So Lewis," Maple began on a curious note, "still feeling uncertain about yourself?"

"Some." Lewis hesitated. "Actually, a lot."

"Hmmm," hemmed Maple. "If you can find the words, Lewis, and you're up to the effort, describe your uncertainties. How do they feel?"

Lewis knew Mrs. Baderhoovenlisterah rarely posed idle questions. When she sought a direct answer from someone, it was usually because she already understood the matter and was preparing to disseminate her knowledge. Lewis admired this about her and replied as honestly as possible. "To begin with, it feels wrong to be uncertain. After that, well, lately I've been having fits where it's difficult to breathe. Nothing too serious, but definitely uncomfortable."

"What kind of fits, exactly?"

"Chest fits, I think. Or maybe my lungs. It's hard to say. It's one part gripping sensation, and one part tingling . . . all over my upper body. It's hard to breathe when they come. Sort of feels as if I'm wearing a wet shirt that's a size too small for me."

"Aha." A bell rang in Maple's head.

"You know the feeling?"

"Sure, I know it. The undersized-wet-shirt syndrome is a classic."

Lewis eyed Maple, wondering if she was pulling his leg.

She was not. "Generally speaking, the tingling begins in the cerebrum above the parietal lobe, near the top of your noggin, then it floods down the medulla oblongata, seeps into the neck and through the shoulders, and ultimately restricts the muscles around the chest."

Lewis was astonished. "That's exactly how it feels. Wow. Are you saying it's all in my head?"

"No. I'm saying it starts in your head. Once it works into the chest, however, it's very real. It's called an identity crisis. They are nothing to sneeze at — everyone knows it hurts being a stranger to yourself — but they are easy to cure."

"They are? How?"

Maple ate a forkful of casserole before answering, "You must relax, Lewis. Identity crises feed on attention. The less one worries about them, the quicker they go away."

Lewis was speechless and all ears.

"*Who* you are, Lewis, is not carved in stone. It's a flexible concept. Your identity is an outgrowth of what you think, and what you think, of course, determines what you believe, which in turn colors your dreams, all of which influence the story you tell with your life."

"I, ah . . . excuse me for being dim, Mrs.

Baderhoovenlisterah, but I don't follow. When you say 'story,' do you mean like in a book?"

Maple chortled. "A book is a good place to look for a story, but what I meant was, life is a strange journey from birth to death, and for most people, that journey is easier understood as a story. It can be religious, or historic, or personal. Whatever. The point is, the journey of life is best understood within a context, and each individual creates his or her own. Indeed, that's the beauty of our universe. You get to choose the story you tell."

Lewis nodded. He was deep in thought.

"A little secret here," Maple added. "If you relax while choosing your story and don't worry about precisely defining yourself, your chest-gripping episodes will cease."

"Just like that?" Lewis wondered excitedly. "I choose a story to tell with my life and I'm better?"

"No," said Maple. "Life is never 'just like that.' It's more complicated. It's . . . well, life is essentially all about change, and there are three basic kinds of change. First you have gradual change. It slowly alters circumstances and transforms the individual by degrees. Then there are out-of-the-blue changes. They turn everything abruptly around and test one's adaptability. Lastly, there are inspired changes, my favorite. They bring an improved way of understanding what you already know." Maple paused to look in Lewis's eyes and confirm that he was still with her. "The out-of-the-blue changes are the tricky ones. You have to watch them, as they usually mark a major turning point in your life. I call them plot-twisters."

Lewis paused for a moment. "Thanks for telling me this, Mrs. Baderhoovenlisterah."

"You're most welcome."

"One more question, if you don't mind. Are you telling a story with your life?"

Maple leaned back and cackled. "You're darn tootin', young man. I'm telling an epic, I hope."

FOUR

Lewis suffered no breathing fits in the days and nights following his conversation with Mrs. Baderhoovenlisterah. Bit by bit he began to relax about his uncertain identity . . . and was soon feeling like his ordinary self again. So what if he didn't know his biological mother or father? Big deal. Worse things had happened to other people. He had interesting friends, good health, loving parents, and a comfortable home to live in. He also (possibly) knew where the biggest trout in all of Idaho could be caught.

In due course, he began entertaining ideas for the telling of his life story. If he understood Maple's concept correctly — and he thought he did — the components of his personal narrative were out there waiting for him to invent. All he had to do was think of what he believed, have dreams, and decide upon a plot to follow. He had fun considering the possibilities: Lewis Hinton, senator of Idaho. Lewis, the music promoter who gave Amanda Dot her first contract. Or perhaps host of the popular television show, *Landing the Big One with Lewis.*

He enjoyed himself in this creative manner . . . until halfway through dinner on Wednesday night when Martha peered dotingly across the table and said, "So, son, you turn sixteen on Saturday. How do you feel about becoming a young man?"

Lewis smiled thinly at his mother. "I thought I was one."

"You are," Martha conceded, "but not completely until your sixteenth birthday. I believe that's the tradition." Martha glanced at Avery, who shrugged neutrally. She took the gesture as an endorsement and resumed. "There is a special surprise that I've been saving until you turn sixteen. Becoming a young man is a major turning point in one's life."

Lewis stiffened in his seat. It troubled him

that Martha said "major turning point." Those were the exact words Mrs. Baderhoovenlisterah had used when warning him about out-of-the-blue changes. Was "major turning point" a common expression amongst older people? he wondered. Had he allowed himself to be inspired by a cliché?

"Are you all right, son?"

"I'm okay."

No one spoke for a moment. Finally, Martha said, "Is there anything special you'd like for dinner on Saturday? I know you're fond of scalloped potatoes. I was thinking of making them and roasting a chicken. And, of course, baking an angel food cake."

"That'll be great, Mom," Lewis placidly agreed, then excused himself to his room, where he lay on his bed and stared blankly at the ceiling. He was disappointed with himself for being so gullible, ashamed at having been inspired by the clichés of an eccentric old woman. Downward he sank into a quagmire of personal doubts, and was soon reduced to thinking, *I'm an idiot for taking Mrs. Baderhoovenlisterah so seriously. Everyone knows she is kooky. Plot-twisters. Life is a story. Three kinds of change. Yeah, right. I can't believe I fell for that.*

Lewis was back in full crisis by Thursday afternoon. He was sitting in study hall, trying to concentrate, when Amanda tiptoed forward and finger-flicked the tip of his left ear. He jolted upright, undulated in his seat, whirled around, and shot daggers from his eyes.

Amanda giggled. "Excuse me. I didn't know you had a 'GO' button on your ear."

Lewis replied through clenched teeth, "You'll have a 'STOP' button on your nose if you aren't careful."

"Now, now." Amanda sat at the desk behind Lewis and pulled a math book from her bag. "So, this coming Saturday is the twelfth. Misty and I are making plans."

Lewis faced the front of the room and

pretended he didn't know the significance of the twelfth. "Plans for what?"

"Your birthday party."

"Oh, that. I'm not having a party."

"Don't be absurd. Everyone celebrates their sixteenth birthday. It's a mandate."

"Listen, Amanda," Lewis said pointedly. "My birthday could be anytime between now and last Christmas. The twelfth means nothing to me. You have a party if you want, but I'm not coming."

"No, you listen," Amanda replied with equal precision. "We are celebrating your birthday on Saturday night, even if it's just the gang sitting around doing nothing."

Lewis grit his teeth.

Amanda had a stubborn streak. When she wanted something to happen, she generally did not desist until it did. "You'd be wise to agree with me, Lewis. If you don't, next time I see you I'll do more than flick the tip of your ear."

"GRRR."

"I'm presuming that is a yes."

Lewis sighed wearily and surrendered. "Okay, Amanda. But just the gang."

Lewis wandered to the park after school, sat on a bench, and watched the Little Lost River tumble into the gorge beyond the fence. It was hard for him to imagine he'd been so happy the day before. He had no desire to fish for the trout. He just wanted his troubles to disappear.

He'd been sitting over an hour when he heard the afternoon whistle at the Slippery Falls Footstool and Ladder Factory. Twelve minutes later, Avery passed by the park on his way home from work and saw Lewis sitting on the bench. Avery parked his car, got out, and walked to the bench. "Hey, son. Mind a little company?"

"Of course not, Dad."

Avery sat and admired the waterfall for a moment, then cleared his throat to speak.

"I don't know what's bothering you, Lewis, but you've been up and down a lot lately. Is something wrong?"

Lewis looked solemn. He was not proud of his confusion, nor did he enjoy troubling his father. "I, ah . . . I guess I have been in a funk lately. I'm sorry."

"Want to talk about it? Your poor mother has been worrying herself silly about you."

"She hearing that voice again?"

Avery shook his head. "No. This worry comes from her heart. I feel it, too, Lewis. You don't seem happy . . . and that disturbs us. You're too young to have problems. At your age, you should be out there kicking up your heels."

Lewis moaned.

"Try talking to me, son. I want to understand."

Lewis paused to collect himself. "Please don't take this wrong — you and Mom are great. You really are — but the fact is, Dad, I've never gotten over learning I was found on Hidden Lane."

Avery replied so softly, Lewis almost did not hear. "Given. Not found."

Lewis bit his bottom lip.

Avery leaned forward and clasped his hands. His face bespoke internal debate, then sudden resolution, and he said, "You should know this, son. After Martha and I were married, we tried for years to have children. Being a mother was all Martha asked. It was all she wanted . . . yet for some reason, no babies came. It was hard on the two of us, and I carried around our failure like a weight. Then the day came when I went walking and you were presented to me. That day, Lewis, was a glorious day for your mother and me. You may be confused about who you are, but Martha and I have no doubts. You are the miracle we were waiting for."

Lewis struggled through a diversity of emotions. "I've never felt anything but wanted and loved by you and Mom. Being your son has nothing to do with my moodiness. It's something else that's getting me . . . an almost physical curiosity about where I come from, about who my real parents are. I wish I could shake it, but I can't. It's there every day when I wake up."

Avery nodded. He understood. "I don't know if this will help matters, Lewis, but between us — not for Martha's ears — the woman who gave me the basket was the prettiest, most intelligent-looking woman I've ever seen. She had your gray-blue eyes, and although she was obviously very sad to give you away, she seemed to know exactly what she was doing and why. When she spoke to me, I sensed she had a noble heart."

"Do you mean proud?"

"Maybe. More, I was thinking, noble like majestic. You know, someone with a refined spirit."

"Oh."

Avery unclasped his hands and sat up. A far-off look entered his eyes, and the expression on his face said he was trying to remember something. Lewis watched Avery struggle with his memory for a moment, then concede defeat. Whatever he'd been trying to recall was gone. A new thought reshaped the lines of his face. He sighed and said, "It's strange, Lewis. All these years and I've never been able to figure what your birth mother was doing on Hidden Lane. How she got there, or why — it's beyond my guessing. All I know is that she seemed a long, long way from home."

Lewis fought off a cry. "You told me once that she spoke with a foreign accent."

"She did." Avery looked off into space for a few seconds and struggled to recall a moment that had passed many years ago. Then he shook his head and said, "I'm glad we had this talk, son."

"Me, too," Lewis agreed. He thought it unlikely that anyone anywhere had a kinder, more decent father.

Avery stood up slowly from the bench. "I'm sure you'll feel better soon. See you at home for supper?"

"You bet, Dad." Lewis watched with thoughtful affection as Avery strolled across the park and got in his car. Then Lewis returned his attention to the gushing curtain of water that was Slippery Falls . . . and heard it whisper, *Whooorrruuu? Whooorrruuu?*

FiVE

Lewis was on his sitting rock by nine-thirty on Saturday morning, the day of his supposed birthday. Although he remained bogged in the doubtful quagmire into which he had fallen midweek, a brightly shining sun lifted his spirits to the point where he could imagine catching the giant trout.

If imagining something can make it happen, Lewis would have caught the big trout, paraded it past the doubters on the bridge, and gloated as they marveled over his triumph. Imagining, in this case, however, amounted mostly to wishing — and wishing, for all its positive attributes, evidently will not incite a fish to strike a lure it doesn't want to strike.

Lewis reeled in his line at quarter past five and started for home. He'd promised Martha he would be showered, dressed, and ready to eat by six o'clock. He was also mildly curious about the surprise she had mentioned earlier in the week.

Since it was a special occasion, the Hintons ate in the dining room. No one said much during the meal, after which Martha took the dinner plates into the kitchen. She returned with a platter balanced on the fingertips of her right hand. Atop the platter was an angel food cake. In her left hand was a rope basket.

The instant Lewis saw the basket he knew something profound was about to happen. He'd grown up seeing the homemade vessel stashed on a shelf in Martha's sewing nook, and for the last year of his life had known it was the craft Avery brought him home in.

As for Avery, his jaw dropped and his eyes flashed with anticipation. He had suddenly recalled a fact that had lain idle in the back of his mind for many years: the letter.

Martha set the platter on the table and the basket on the floor, then cut and served everyone a slice of angel food cake. No one spoke while they ate their cake. Only chewing and swallowing sounds permeated the room.

The clinking of forks being set on empty plates brought an end to the awkward silence. Finally, the time had come for Martha to deliver the speech she had drafted and redrafted in her head throughout so many long nights during the past sixteen years. She cleared her throat and announced, "You are a man now. I've been keeping something for you since you were an infant. I found it under the blankets in this basket at my side. I believe it's a letter. I have not opened it to look." Martha reached down and removed a time-yellowed envelope from the basket. Gazing directly into Lewis's eyes, she extended the mysterious missive across the table. Before releasing it into Lewis's outstretched hand, she said, "I ask only one thing from you, son. When you read whatever is written here, remember that neither Avery nor I would have given you away for all the world. Never in a quadrillion years."

"I know you wouldn't abandon me," Lewis said weakly.

Martha released the envelope from her clasp, nodded to Avery, and arose from her chair. Avery, understanding her intent, stood and followed his wife from the room.

Lewis read the words printed on the envelope: GIVE WHEN LITTLE MAN. These four words comprised the first communication he'd ever received from his biological mother. Or at least he assumed his mother had written the words. There was one way to find out. He tore open the envelope.

Lewis's heart sank when he saw the length of the letter. It amounted to a single paragraph, printed in blue ink on cream-colored paper.

LOUIS,

MY BEAUTIFUL BOY. I SPEAK YOU IN ENGLISH, WHICH IS THE TONGUE YOU SPEAK NOW. NOT MY BEST

SPEAKING. I HOPE YOU GLAD FOR THE LIFE YOU HAVE. I WAS NOT CONTENT TO SAY GOOD-BYE. I MEET WITH HARD TIME IN UNITED STATES. MUST BE FREE TO FIND YOUR FATHER. HE BEHAVES ME LIKE A QUEEN. WE WISH THAT YOU GROW IN GOOD PLACE. I SEE NICE MAN WALKING. I WAIT AND GIVE YOU HIM. PLEASE KNOW I LEAVE YOU WITH MY PRAYERS.

J. A. POISSON

Lewis reread the letter and sat numbly for a moment. Then it hit him. He knew his name. His name was Louis Poisson. He wasn't sure how to pronounce it, but it was his *name*.

His mother had called him a beautiful boy. She had left him to find his father, her husband, who treated her like a queen. He was Louis.

Lewis drew a breath. Rather than think, he felt thoughts rising up in him.

To Martha, waiting just outside the door, the dining room was quiet for an awfully long time. So long, she could no longer restrain herself and tapped lightly. "Are you okay in there?"

"I'm fine."

"Glad to hear it."

Lewis snorted with amusement. "Come in, Mom. Dad, too."

Martha and Avery sat at the table across from Lewis and waited. Lewis held up the letter and offered, "Just so you know, before you read this, I would never forget who my real mom and dad are. You are the parents I know."

Martha almost cried. Avery beamed with pride. "Thank you for saying so, son."

Lewis handed the letter across the table. Martha unfolded the paper and — with Avery peeking from the side — read the words that had been in her keep for so many long years. When she was done, she laid the letter on the table, looked closely at Avery, and kissed his cheek, then turned and told Lewis, "Anyone who would trade a child for freedom doesn't deserve to be a mother. We all should be glad that woman gave you up."

Martha's comment took Lewis by surprise.

He'd never thought of it that way — of his birth mother making a choice when she gave him to Avery. A flash of resentment shot through Lewis. Martha was right. J. A. Poisson had elected to put him in the basket and run off to find his father.

Lewis's anger faded as fast as it appeared. He'd never been bitter about his circumstances, just emotionally uncertain. He reminded Martha, "She says in her letter that she was having a hard time. I don't hold what my mother did against her, and neither should you, Mom."

"You are absolutely correct," Martha agreed with alacrity. "It was wrong of me to impugn your mother without ever walking in her shoes. I'm sure she is a very upstanding person."

The word "is" resonated loudly in Lewis's mind. "Is" implied that J. A. Poisson was currently living somewhere. That she was almost certainly alive.

"You do forgive me, don't you, Lewis?"

"Of course I do, Mom."

Avery chose this moment to stand and take a bill from his wallet, which he extended to Lewis. "Happy birthday."

Lewis was impressed. "You don't have to give me that much."

"I don't," Avery agreed. "But you have to take it."

Lewis grinned. "Thanks, Dad. You, too, Mom. Thank you both."

"You're welcome," Martha and Avery chimed.

Lewis took the letter and the fifty to his bedroom. He reread the letter, stuck it and the fifty in a dictionary on his desk, and flopped across his bed. His senses were heightened, his mind on full alert. He felt a change taking place within him. It was too soon for him to comprehend the exact nature of the change, yet he knew without a doubt that he had reached some kind of major turning point in his life.

At quarter to eight, he hopped off the bed and threw on a jacket. He had a birthday party to attend, and for the first time in a while, Lewis was genuinely eager for the good company of his friends.

He was heading down Main Street when he noticed a light shining in Mrs. Baderhoovenlisterah's library. Pausing to study the house, he felt a stab of regret for having doubted the woman's character. Sure, she was an eccentric, but that didn't prevent her from having wisdom to impart . . . or from being a living epic who had accurately ascertained the source of his breathing fits and prescribed a cure that had thus far proved effective.

Lewis resumed walking. As he passed by the park he composed a ditty that he sang in his head. "I have a name. I found my past. I know who I am at last."

SiX

Amanda and Misty were waiting on the sidewalk in front of Chip's when Lewis arrived. Misty, wearing a maroon beret, carried supplies for the campfire that was planned on the far side of the river. "Happy birthday," said Amanda, stepping forward and kissing Lewis quickly on the cheek. "I know, I know. We're not supposed to make a big deal about it. I just had to say it once."

"It's fine with me," replied Lewis. He was wishing Amanda would kiss him more often.

"Fine? Really? I thought you were stressed about your birthday."

Lewis shrugged. "Yeah, maybe I was. Still, if you want to wish me a happy one again, I don't mind."

Amanda stepped back and eyed Lewis sharply. Something about him was different. She could smell it, even if she couldn't put her finger on what had changed. She glanced at

Misty to see if she noticed anything different. Misty's perplexed expression suggested she did. Amanda looked back at Lewis. His serene smile confirmed Amanda's suspicion. "Something happened," she stated matter-of-factly. "You caught your big fish, didn't you?"

"No."

"What, then? I can see it in your face, Lewis. You have obviously changed."

Lewis frowned and pretended not to know what Amanda was talking about.

"Don't play games with me," she commanded.

"Me? Play games?"

"You're playing one now, Lewis. Do you think I can't see through you?"

Lewis was amused. "I don't put anything past you."

Misty started walking. "Come on. You guys can fight later. Gaston and Sophie and Lob should have a fire going by now."

Amanda and Lewis fell into step behind

Misty. They'd gone less than twenty yards when she observed darkly, "You either fell and bruised your brain, or something important happened. I want to know what's up. You have to tell me."

They proceeded to the one bridge that spanned the Little Lost and connected the town of Slippery Falls with the outside world. The structure was three hundred yards long and suspended approximately forty feet above the water. As the trio made their way to the other side, a waxing moon — two nights shy of full — bathed the river gorge in a soft silvery light. In typical springtime fashion, the Little Lost was swollen to the brink with snowmelt.

Lewis veered to the guardrail and stared at the moonlit waterfall. Amanda joined him, and they admired the scene together for several seconds. Then Amanda said, "Here we are, on a bridge over troubled waters. A good time and place for sharing secrets."

"I'm surprised you haven't figured it out," noted Lewis.

Amanda wrinkled her brow and figured as fast as she could.

Misty grew tired of waiting in the road and called, "I'm going ahead. See you guys at the campfire."

"Be there in a minute," replied Amanda, who stared intensely at Lewis. Suddenly, it dawned on her. "You found out who you are, didn't you?"

"More or less. I learned my name."

"What? How'd you find out?"

"I'll tell you after we join the others. They'll want to hear as well, I'm sure."

Beyond the bridge on the left side of the road lay a narrow deer path that ran north through a patch of woods. The path led to an open, boulder-strewn field nestled between a range of rugged hills and the river gorge. In the middle of the field, a bowl-shaped depression formed a sort of natural amphitheater that was ideal for a campfire.

They'd hardly reached the fire site and said hello to the others before Amanda clapped her hands and commanded, "Listen up. Lewis has important news."

Lewis looked at everyone and grew thoughtful.

When, after ten seconds, he still hadn't spoken, Amanda told him tersely, "We're all friends here, Lewis, which means we've been tolerating your glum presence for nearly a year now. You owe us the facts."

"Yeah," said Lob. "What's the deal?"

Lewis leaned forward and rested his elbows on his knees. The fire crackled and flickered shadows across the attentive faces of his friends. "I learned my name," he told them after a pause.

"And?" Amanda prompted.

"Who are you?" wondered Gaston.

Lewis explained about the letter and informed the group, "My first name is still Lewis, only it's spelled L-O-U-I-S. My last name, I'm not sure how to pronounce. It's spelled P-O-I-S-S-O-N."

"Poison?" Lob suggested.

"Yuck. Poison is a terrible name," blurted Misty. After Amanda rebuked her with a look, she amended, "Actually, for a last name, it's not bad. Kind of interesting, really."

Silence fell over the group, and for a moment, even the fire was quiet. Then Sophie said, "The name is pronounced Pwah-sawn. It's French."

"French?" Lewis was intensely curious. "Are you sure?"

"Oui," Sophie answered. "Remember, I moved here from Montreal when I was eight. I grew up speaking French."

Lewis nodded. "And you're sure it's a French name?"

"Pretty sure. In French, the word *poisson* means 'fish.'"

Lewis drew a sharp breath and stared pensively into the fire. Everyone watched him for a reaction . . . and a look of bemused wonder soon appeared on his face. "Who would have thunk," he mused glibly. "I'm French."

Lob threw back his head and roared, "You're a frog."

"No, Lob," Gaston countered. "He's a fish."

Misty guffawed. "That explains everything!"

Sophie giggled.

"Children!" Amanda barked imperiously. "Control yourselves. This is serious." But no one obeyed Amanda's directive. Not even her, who soon trembled with glee and cried, "Misty, lend Lewis your beret. Let's see how it looks on him."

"Here." Misty handed her hat to Lewis. "I give this to you for your birthday."

Lewis put on the maroon chapeau and struck a pose. Although not as amused as his friends, he did not begrudge their laughing.

In due course, the group quit dwelling on Lewis and shifted their attention to other, more incidental, matters. A short while later, Lewis excused himself to go pee. He walked to the bluffs overlooking the river and peered across the gorge to the moonlit cliffs below the park. Some two hundred yards to his left lay the bridge. Half that distance to his right, the Little Lost spilled from its high plateau.

When Lewis was done with his business, he slipped off his shoes and — undaunted by the unfamiliar terrain here on the west side of the river — headed toward Slippery Falls. He let his feet pick a path, and they carried him to a mound of boulders on the bluffs beside the waterfall. The uppermost boulder reached to within a foot or so of the river's fluid lip. Without hesitating, Lewis climbed the mound and ascended to the rocky summit.

The view was magnificent, accompanied by the symphonic gush of the tumbling Little Lost. Lewis was entranced. Never had he stood so near the waterfall, nor so intimately felt its power.

Lewis was lost in thought when something caught his eye.

What was that?! A cavern behind the falls?

Compelled by curiosity, and risking the precise kind of disaster that Martha Hinton feared the most, Lewis inched his way onto the outermost arc of boulder and leaned toward the waterfall. He could just barely make out a horizontal fissure in the earthen wall beneath the river. He squinted and strained to see through the dimly lit curtain of water. Be it a cavern or exposed tunnel, or crevice or a crack — there was definitely an opening behind the falls.

A bold line of thought soon formed in Lewis's mind: *If I can get from this boulder into that space, and if it runs to the far side of the gorge as it appears . . . then I could approach the back side of the pool where the giant trout lives. The big fish would not expect a lure from this direction. Hmmm. Just a little luck and I could catch that monster by surprise.*

Lewis was drawn from his reveries by the distant sound of Lob's voice. "Lewis, where are you? I found your shoes, but you're not in them."

Lewis cupped his hands to his mouth and shouted over the roar of the waterfall, "Here."

"Where?"

"I'm coming," Lewis hollered. He took one last look at the cavern, descended the jumble of boulders, and started back along the bluffs. He could hardly believe his luck. A few hours earlier he'd finally learned his name, and now he had a promising new scheme for catching the great-granddaddy trout that had eluded him for the past year.

Lewis and Lob were returning to the fire site when Lewis's cheerful mood suffered a deflating blow. Amanda and Gaston were side by side on a rock with their heads inclined toward each other in intimate conversation. As they spoke, Amanda reached over and placed a hand on Gaston's knee.

Lewis suppressed a breathing fit and quietly sang the jingle he'd composed earlier that evening: "I have a name. I found my past. I know who I am at last."

SEVEN

Lewis slept deeper on Saturday night than he'd slept in a year and did not rise from bed until quarter of eleven the next morning. He found Martha and Avery in the living room, dressed for church, which they attended regularly and Lewis attended on occasion. After good mornings were exchanged, Lewis announced, "There's something I want to tell you."

Martha glanced at a clock. "We leave in five minutes."

"It'll only take a second," Lewis replied, then proceeded to share what he'd learned about his other name.

Martha paused to consider, allowing Avery to comment on the matter before she did. He did so affably. "French, you say. I reckon you'll be wanting to grow one of those little mustaches now."

"Excuse me, Dad," Lewis said gently, "but

I believe you are thinking of an Italian gondolier."

"That may be," Avery conceded. "Still, if you want to grow fuzz on your lip, it wouldn't offend me."

Martha coughed. She was ready to weigh in, and did. "The French are controversial. However, they sold us Louisiana for a bargain price and helped George Washington win the American Revolution, so they can't be all bad."

Lewis stared in amazement at Martha. There was no predicting what the woman might say.

Soon after Martha and Avery departed, Lewis headed toward Mrs. Baderhoovenlisterah's house. As luck would have it (or maybe it was something more than luck), she was standing in her front doorway when he arrived at the gate. "In the mood for company?" Lewis asked after saying hello.

"Come in, come in."

They went into the library, where Lewis sat on a stool while Maple stood opposite him, leaning against a bookshelf. Lewis could feel her listening even before he began to speak. "Remember I told you how I was given to my father in a basket by a strange woman on Hidden Lane?"

Maple nodded. "Sweet story, like a fairy tale."

"Well," Lewis began. "The woman who gave me away — my natural mother — wrote a letter that she put in the basket with me. My mom — Martha — found it hidden under some blankets and saved it for me until my sixteenth birthday, which we celebrated last night."

"Happy birthday. What did the letter say?"

Lewis removed the yellowed envelope from his hip pocket and handed it to Maple.

She read the missive, glanced at the ceiling, looked at Lewis, and scrutinized the signature on the letter. "Hmm. Poisson. That name rings a bell. Definitely French. Now let me see." Maple reached up to tap her temple with an index finger. "I believe that was . . . now, come on, thought, I know you're in there."

Lewis leaned forward, a look of encouragement on his face.

"I wonder . . ." Maple continued. "J. A. Poisson. Does it have to do . . . was it the maiden name of . . . who? Durn. I can't quite remember."

Lewis was overwhelmed with curiosity. "You can do it, Mrs. Baderhoovenlisterah. Maiden name of who? Just say the answer."

Maple skewered her face into a pout and strained her brain to its considerable limits. For a brief few seconds she appeared to tug on a promising lead . . . but it got away, and she said, "Sorry, Lewis. My noggin has gone on strike. I'm going to need to hit the books and jog some memories loose. That might take awhile. Best you leave me now and check back in a couple of hours."

Lewis did as Maple suggested. He'd waited this long — what was a couple of more hours? In fact, it was about the length of time he figured he would need to cross the river and reconnoiter the recently discovered cavern.

Upon climbing the boulders by the falls on the east side of the gorge, Lewis saw two sobering details he had not noticed the night before. For one thing, a line of tooth-shaped stones hugged the riverbank at the base of the bluffs, some two hundred feet below him. There was no doubt that an accidental plummet from the boulders would result in sudden death. Lewis also saw that the gap between him and the cavern was nearly twelve feet wide, as well as interrupted by a thick wall of falling water.

Discouraged but not defeated, Lewis studied the situation for the next ninety minutes, seeking a solution that did not come until after he descended the boulders and started back along the crest of the bluffs. He was about halfway between the falls and the bridge when a notion pressed upon the roof of his cerebellum. It was a visual notion, which he patiently allowed to take shape. He saw a ladder. A lightweight, aluminum ladder with a broad base and narrow top. It was horizontal in the air, with its base anchored atop a boulder, its midsection extended through a curtain of water, and its tip projecting into a cavern.

Lewis shook a fist over his head. He had a plan. He knew it was a dubious plan, but it was a plan nonetheless, and . . . well, he just happened to live in a town where ladders of all shapes and sizes were readily available.

Lewis found Mrs. Baderhoovenlisterah sitting cross-legged on the library floor with books scattered all around her. She looked up as he entered and directed him with a glance to sit. After he did, she said, "I found what I was looking for."

"That's good," Lewis said a little nervously.

Maple nodded and continued. "If I may, Lewis, a word to the wise before I tell you what I found. While allowing that *who* is a flexible concept and that you should tell whatever story you wish with your life, please keep in mind that moderation is a virtue, even in the realms of imagination."

"I'll keep it in mind," Lewis agreed, not sure why Maple said what she did.

She saw his confusion and explained. "Essentially, Lewis, I'm advising you against my own penchants. You see, ever since I was a little girl, I've tended to elaborate on the known truth. My mother called it plausibility stretching. She said it was in my blood, and only transfusion would cure me."

Lewis thought, *Whoever heard of plausibility stretching?* He offered politely, "I've always thought you were realistic."

"Real, perhaps," Maple rebutted, "although I wouldn't bet on the istic part. Anyhow, I'm only asking that you keep a little perspective when I tell you about the marquise."

"The what?"

"Marquise. A noblewoman of hereditary rank in France. It's roughly equivalent to a duchess in England. The woman I was trying to remember was a marquise named Jeanne Antoinette Poisson. J. A. Poisson, just like your mother."

"Wow. And she was French?"

"As French as they come. Jeanne Antoinette Poisson was her name at birth, before she was known to the world as Madame de Pompadour. She just happened to have been the smartest, most sophisticated woman of the eighteenth century. She was a truly amazing individual. She had a lovely singing voice, was an accomplished painter, a talented actor, and had a genuine knack for governing. And as if that wasn't enough for one person, she was also quite beautiful."

Lewis was too overwhelmed to speak.

Maple was enjoying herself. "Madame de Pompadour more or less ran France during the reign of King Louis the Fifteenth. He made her a marquise. They were in love for many, many years."

"King Louis," Lewis whispered incredulously. "A woman named J. A. Poisson was the lover of a king named Louis?"

"Indeed. Of course, most of the kings in France were named Louis. The Fifteenth was an okay fellow, but not what anyone would call a hard worker. He inherited the throne as a child of five and grew up rather spoiled. He was, however, wise enough to listen to Madame de Pompadour's advice on political matters. Some historians claim he relied on her too much. Others insist he should have listened to her more."

Lewis shook his head. He was taking everything in, but had no idea what to make of it.

Maple picked up three books from a pile beside her and presented them to Lewis. "I anticipated that you'd be curious, and selected a few titles that will tell you more about Madame de Pompadour and King Louis, and the fascinating times in which they lived. Keep the books as long as you want. I put your letter in the one on top."

Lewis hopped off the stool and picked up the books. "Thank you, Mrs. Baderhoovenlisterah. I'll read these straightaway. I have one question, though, if you don't mind."

"Not at all."

"Jeanne Antoinette Poisson," Lewis pronounced the name carefully. "Was she the woman who said, 'Let them eat cake' and had her head cut off by a mob?"

Maple grinned. "No. That was Marie Antoinette, the wife of King Louis the Sixteenth. She was an actual queen."

"Oh." Lewis was relieved, and excited. "I'm sure glad I brought the letter for you to read. I never would have made the link on my own."

"Never eliminates all possibility."

"Well, I probably wouldn't have made the connection," Lewis reiterated. "Anyway, thanks for the information. I really appreciate it, I do."

"It's my pleasure sharing knowledge."

"I know, and that's lucky for me. I'm going to go now, Mrs. Baderhoovenlisterah. It was great talking with you."

"Ditto, Lewis. Anytime. And remember what I said about keeping your sense of perspective, okay?"

EiGHT

Back home Lewis stared at the bound texts with a mixture of apprehension and thrill, all but certain they held critical clues to his identity. Why else, he reasoned, would Maple have advised him to moderate his imagination when telling his personal story? Evidently, there was information in the books that linked Lewis to a royal past.

Martha and Avery were taking their customary Sunday nap together and the house was silent. Lewis reached and touched the top book . . . and hesitated. Several indecisive moments passed, then he turned and walked from the room. *The truth could wait,* he reflected. Just now he hankered for a pause in the rapid flow of change that had been taking place within him since the evening before. He was in need of a familiar routine.

He grabbed his fishing gear from the garage and headed toward the park. He climbed the iron fence, made his way across the cliff, settled on his sitting rock, checked the lead on his lure, drew back his pole, and cast his line into the tumultuous face of Slippery Falls. He propped the butt of his pole against the rock and held the tip out over the gorge.

Lewis appeared to be fishing, but he was not — not in the true, praying-for-a-strike meaning of the word. He was only going through the motions, for inwardly he was busy reviewing the various pieces of personal information that had been revealed to him in the past twenty or so hours of his life.

Lewis could feel the undigested data mixing inside of him . . . blending and becoming part of him . . . reshaping and redefining the very concept of who he was. Emotions, old and new, arose and fell of their own volition. All the while, the falling Little Lost wanted to know, *Whooorrruuu? Whooorrruu?*

Ideas, riding impulses, shot through his mind.

My mother gave me to a complete stranger, just as someone would give away a puppy. In sixteen years, one lousy letter.

Mom and Dad kept me as one of their own. They would never give me away.

The French are controversial. Oooh, Martha. That's funny.

Mine is not a bizarre story. It's different, that's all.

The ideas soon ceased coming and were replaced with wordless feelings. Lulled by the sonorous gush of the river, Lewis slipped out of time and drifted slowly into a trancelike state of being. He was just someone sitting on a rock in the sun. Fortunately, the giant trout did not choose this day and hour to strike Lewis's silver lure, for if it had done so, the fish would have surely caught the fisherman.

After who knows how long, Lewis heard — or thought he heard — a voice whisper, "Louis."

He blinked and looked around. There was no one in sight.

"Louis." The waterfall murmured in a woman's voice. A voice with a foreign accent, no less?

Lewis listened with all his might.

"Louis, I am so sorry for the pain I caused you. Yet you must know, I have feelings, too. Giving you to the man on Hidden Lane made me very sad. It was an impossible decision. I was doing for you what I thought best."

Then, as mysteriously as it had arisen, the voice fell silent. There was only the river.

Lewis continued sitting perfectly still, listening inside and out of himself. What came next was a sensation, not a voice. It was a warm and tingling sensation that started in his heart, spread through his chest and shoulders, surged up his medulla oblongata, and into his cerebellum. Metaphysically, it was the opposite of an undersized-wet-shirt attack.

He sat a spell longer, then, before reeling in his line and heading for home, filled his chest with air and shouted into the gorge,

"Jeanne Antoinette Poisson, wherever you might be, I hope you are happy and my father behaves you like a queen."

Lewis was heading up Main Street when he saw Sophie Joilet coming out the front door of Mrs. Baderhoovenlisterah's house. They waved to each other and met at the gate. Lewis saw that Sophie was carrying a book and asked, "What'cha got there?"

"A biography on Catherine the Great."

Lewis drew a blank.

"She ruled Russia for many years in the eighteenth century," Sophie volunteered, then added with a wry smile, "Before becoming the czarina, she was a princess named Sophie."

Lewis grew profoundly curious. The coincidence of both he and Sophie being named after eighteenth-century rulers struck him as odd, to say the least, and he asked, "Did you pick that book out, or did Mrs. Baderhoovenlisterah recommend it to you?"

"Yes and no," Sophie equivocated. "I mean, I asked her for a suggestion. She just reached onto a shelf beside where she was standing and picked this book."

Lewis hemmed thoughtfully and a little bit suspiciously. Was Mrs. Baderhoovenlisterah's penchant for plausibility stretching prompting her to turn everyone from Slippery Falls into royalty?

"I don't know what you're thinking, Lewis, but I'm fond of biographies. I read two or three of them a month."

"You do?"

"Yes. I find it interesting reading about people's lives, about what happens to them and how they respond."

Lewis studied Sophie closely for several seconds. "When you say 'what happens to them and how they respond,' do you mean that people tell stories with their lives?"

Sophie shrugged. "I hadn't thought of it that way before, but now that you mention it, yes, I suppose people do tell stories with their lives. That's a good way of putting it."

"Thanks," Lewis said meekly, aware the compliment actually belonged to Mrs. Baderhoovenlisterah. He was also aware that it was almost six o'clock and Martha would be mad if he wasn't home in time for dinner. Plus, he felt suddenly eager to dive into the books on the table by his bed. "See ya, Sophie. I gotta go. Enjoy your book."

"*Au revoir*, Louis Poisson Hinton."

NINE

Lewis went straight from the dinner table into his room, sat on his bed, and picked up one of the books Maple had lent him. He flipped it open and came by chance to the image of an elegantly dressed, refined-looking woman standing by a harpsichord in a luxurious parlor. A caption beneath the picture informed Lewis that it was a photographic reproduction of an oil painting by François Boucher. The model for the painting was Madame de Pompadour.

Below the painting was a description excerpted from the memoirs of Dufort de Cheverny. Lewis didn't know who Dufort was, but the man had written about Madame de Pompadour: "tall, though not too tall; beautiful figure; round face with regular features; wonderful complexion, hands, and arms; eyes not so very big, but the brightest, wittiest, most sparkling I ever saw. She absolutely extinguished all other women at court, although some were very beautiful."

Lewis returned his attention to the picture. There was nothing glamorous or spectacular about Madame de Pompadour's face, yet in a quiet and serene way she was indeed beautiful. The painter had captured a sweet, innocent expression on his model's face . . . and a twinkling in her eyes gave Lewis the impression that she was a kind, loving person.

Her eyes fascinated Lewis. How much of their allure came from Madame de Pompadour or was the invention of the artist, Lewis would never know, but the gaze in the painting was of a confident, intelligent person. Lewis looked for a hidden message in the eyes . . . hoping to find something that would tell him if he was related to this elegant woman with the same initials and last name as his biological mother.

Why not? Everyone descends from someone. Was it stretching the truth too far to suggest that Lewis was the offspring of the offspring of the offspring of the offspring of the offspring of the offspring of the offspring of Madame de Pompadour and King Louis XV? Lewis did not think so. To him this was a plausible possibility, well within the scope of sound reason.

Lewis closed the book and placed it on the table. He was full to the brim with new knowledge. It had been a long day, and he was tired. He did not bother to undress. He flicked off the light and fell asleep.

He awoke on Monday morning eager to read everything written about Madame de Pompadour. To do so, he had arrangements to make with Martha, whom he found in the kitchen. "Morning, Mom. How are you today?"

"Fairly well. And you?"

Lewis sighed. "I'm not feeling one hundred percent. I think I'd better stay home in bed."

"What's wrong? Do you have a fever?"

"No, not really. I just feel funny."

Martha grew suddenly suspicious. "Funny, you say? Does this have anything to do with your being French?"

"No." Lewis suppressed a grin. "I think my stomach hurts."

"You think?"

Lewis considered for two seconds. "I want to stay home today so I can be close to the most wonderful mom in the world."

Martha snickered. "Well, you obviously aren't fit for appearing in public. I'll write a note for your teachers that says you were feeling funny when you got up on Monday morning."

"Thanks, Mom. You're the best."

Lewis propped himself up with pillows and dove into the stack of books by his bed. Madame de Pompadour and King Louis XV were both interesting characters, to say the least, and in the course of Lewis's reading, many facts lodged themselves prominently in his mind.

Jeanne Antoinette had been married when

she met the king, who invited her to visit his palace at Versailles. As was only proper, she accepted the royal invitation, and during her visit the king was smitten by her graceful charms. Soon afterward, she divorced her husband and King Louis gave her the title of Madame de Pompadour.

She was fond of learning, owned a private library of more than thirty-five hundred volumes, and established herself as the unofficial minister of culture in eighteenth-century France. She was a genius of entertainment who, as a young lady, had been taught to glide across the floor with fast, dainty steps. Frederick the Great called her "Her Petticoat Majesty." Mozart performed for her when he was six years old. She eventually became so famous and admired that her name was given to fans, hairdos, dresses, dishes, ribbons, and the rose color of her favorite porcelain.

King Louis XV had been an orphan without brothers or sisters when he inherited the throne from his grandfather. He grew into a slender but broad-shouldered young man with curly, golden hair and was known to his subjects as "the Well Beloved." King Louis was not above playing on the sympathies of the French people and developed a lifelong habit of falling ill during times of crisis, of which there were many during his reign.

Except for fifteen minutes spent slurping soup at lunchtime, and an occasional trip to the bathroom, Lewis read steadily throughout the day and was still reading at six o'clock when Martha called him for supper. He returned directly to his room after dinner and resumed reading until he flicked off the light at ten fifty-five. By this point Lewis knew more about eighteenth-century France than most of his peers knew about modern-day America.

● ● ●

Lewis, who normally shaved every other day, was doing so on Tuesday morning when — on a whim — he elected to avoid his upper lip with the razor. It was not a big decision, as there currently wasn't enough hair on his lip for anyone to notice. A couple of moments later he was getting dressed in his room when — on another whim — he grabbed the beret Misty had given him and popped it on his head.

Amanda was standing in front of Slippery Falls High when Lewis arrived. "Oh, look," she cooed. "It's the new French guy."

Lewis was not amused. "Good morning, Miss Dot."

"Where were you yesterday?"

"At home in bed. I felt funny."

Amanda rolled her eyes. "Listen, Misty and I want to discuss something with you. Can you meet us at Chip's after school?"

"Sure," Lewis agreed just as the morning bell rang.

"See you then." Amanda blew a little kiss over her shoulder and hurried to her first class.

Barring a few wisecracks about his maroon chapeau, Lewis's school day passed smoothly and relatively swiftly. He was at Chip's before Amanda and Misty, and was waiting in the front booth when they waltzed through the door. They'd hardly settled across from him when Amanda declared, "We've decided. We are going to help you find your mother."

"It's what friends are for," chimed Misty.

"In fact," said Amanda, "the hunt has already begun."

Lewis opened his mouth to speak, but he wasn't quick enough to beat Misty, who announced, "We found eleven J. Poissons on the Internet, all in the U.S. There were no J. A. Poissons."

"It would probably be best to contact them by letter," noted Amanda. "Phone calls might seem too invasive."

Lewis threw up a hand. "Hold it. What makes you think I want to find my birth mother?"

Amanda screwed her eyes at Lewis. "Because you're her son. Why wouldn't you want to find her?"

Lewis grimaced. "Maybe because I have all the mother I need at home. Not to mention that even if I wanted to find J. A. Poisson, she may not want to be found. Besides, she knows where she left me. So let's just leave her be, wherever she is."

Amanda weighed Lewis's words before saying, "Wasn't it last week that you were complaining about not knowing who you were and telling me how important it was to know your ancestors?"

Lewis shrugged.

"Then what happened? Don't you care anymore?"

"Of course I care," Lewis shot back

quickly. "But the way I remember that conversation, Amanda, you were asking questions and I was explaining, not complaining."

"Whatever, Lewis. I refuse to argue over semantics. I only want to help."

"Amanda loves helping people," Misty interjected.

Lewis smiled at Misty and told Amanda, "I don't want to argue, either. Call me confused. Maybe I am. But I have a name now and a past, and for the first time in a long while I'm okay about who I am."

"Fine," Amanda said flatly. "Good."

A strained pause ensued, and then Lewis volunteered, "For what it's worth, I've been reading some fascinating things about the Poisson name."

"What things?" asked Amanda.

"Oh, things like there being a woman named J. A. Poisson who was publicly known as Madame de Pompadour. She practically ran

France during the reign of a king named Louis the Fifteenth."

Amanda's antennae shot up. "Someone with your mother's name was a queen?"

"No, she was a marquise, which is sort of like an appointed princess. She and King Louis were very close."

"Where'd you learn this?" inquired Misty.

"In some books Mrs. Baderhoovenlisterah lent me."

One could see Amanda's mental gears turning as she stared at Lewis. "So your mother has the same name as an appointed princess who was very close to a king named Louis, and they're all from France. Hmm. I find that intriguing. Yes I do."

Misty looked from Lewis to Amanda, then back at Lewis and blurted loudly, "You could be descended from a king! Or at least a princess."

Although Lewis had entertained the exact notion the night before, he did not like the sound of it now. Indeed, hearing the thought broadcast throughout Chip's evoked an ominous stirring in Lewis's stomach. He did what he could to put the cat back in the bag. "Oh, I think that's a stretch. I mean, the names are surely a coincidence. There must be thousands upon thousands of Poissons in France."

Amanda was not diverted from her view. "It could just as easily not be a coincidence, Lewis."

"Yeah," adjoined Misty. "Amazing things happen to some people."

Lewis groaned and slumped down in the booth. He was pretty certain that he'd just been hit by one of those out-of-the-blue plot-twisters Maple had warned him about.

TEN

Amanda and Misty were still waiting for Speedy to come and take their orders when Lewis said good-bye and took off for the bluffs on the far side of the river. He wanted to study the cavern again.

At the foot of the town side of the bridge, Lewis encountered the three most regular members of the regular fishing crowd — the trio who teased Lewis more than everyone else combined. Between them, they represented almost two hundred years of living. Their names were Turly Sweed, Tom Fitzboken, and Hank Maybe. If there can be such a thing as a ringleader among a crowd of three, it was Turly. He waited until Lewis drew even, and remarked, "I'll be durned if it isn't the sky fisherman, come down from his rock."

Lewis kept moving. He had heard it all before.

Hank chortled and quipped, "I reckon the cloud fish aren't biting today."

"Nice lid," said Tom, who was more sensitive and generally easier to take than his associates. "I once had a blue hat like that. Got it in France during the war."

Lewis stopped and turned. "Which war?"

"The Second World War," replied Tom. "You're probably too young to know about that. It was the one where we saved France and the rest of the world from Germany."

"I've heard of that war," said Lewis. "So Mr. Fitzboken, you were in France?"

"Indeed I was."

"What did you think of the place?"

Tom paused to rub the stubble on his chin. "France is a nice enough place, as places go. Probably would've liked it more if I weren't stuck in a trench with people shooting at me."

"Show him your wound, Tom," urged Turly.

Tom looked askance at Turly, then told

Lewis, "Don't worry, son, I'll spare you that excitement."

Lewis grinned and said before departing, "Thanks for the compliment on my hat, Mr. Fitzboken."

Standing on the mound of boulders with his hand over his eyes, Lewis strained to peer through the waterfall and into the cavern. His effort bore little fruit, for he was barely able to see the mouth of the opening, much less visually penetrate its dark recesses. For all he knew, the cavern ended five feet from where it started. He chose not to believe this and instead imagined a tunnel extending westward to the cliffs below the park. It was possible, he mused . . . just as he was possibly a descendant of Madame de Pompadour and King Louis XV.

Lewis removed his shoes, rolled his pants to the knee, sat and clutched the boulder, then projected his right foot into the plunging Little Lost. The first thing he noticed was the downward drive of the river, which was powerful, but not irresistible. Good. The information suggested that an aluminum ladder could withstand the force and weight of the falls. The next thing Lewis noticed was the shockingly low temperature of the water. After a mere ten seconds of exposure, his foot was going numb. This told him that he should wait until late June or early July before attempting to enter the cavern. By then, he figured, the river would be warm enough to survive a quick drenching.

After dressing the next morning, Lewis placed the maroon beret on his head and eyed himself in the mirror. *Pretty smart*, he thought, then thought again, *maybe too smart*. He removed the hat, hung it on the back of a chair, and headed cheerfully off to Slippery Falls High.

Lob Borroughs and a hanger-on named Bennet Field were sitting on the front steps of the school as Lewis arrived. When Lob saw Lewis coming, he popped to his feet, bowed deeply at the waist, and said, "Good morning, Your Majesty."

Before Lewis could ask what Lob was talking about, Bennet stood and solemnly declared, "It's His Royal Highness, Lewis 'Poisson' Hinton."

Lob bowed again and court-rolled his right arm. "At your service, O Illustrious One."

Lewis drew back.

Lob feigned anguish. "Pardon this lowly plebian if I have offended Your Eminence by showing respect."

"Your presence honors us," Bennet added obsequiously.

Lewis didn't have to ask who had filled Lob and Bennet with such nonsense. "Listen, you morons. I'm Lewis Hinton, whom you've known forever. Cut the royal treatment. It's not funny."

"Yes, Your Majesty." Lob grinned. "Whatever you say."

Lewis shook his head and marched away.

Knowing how quickly gossip sometimes spread through Slippery Falls, he feared that Lob and Bennet were just the tip of the iceberg.

His apprehensions were borne out in his first-period Spanish class, where, to his astonishment and surprise, he was greeted with a stern warning look from Miss Krupp. The message in her eyes seemed clear to Lewis: *I know you elitist types. You'd better not stir up any foreign-language troubles for me.*

Lewis took a seat near the back of the room, and after a moment's reflection allowed that he may have imagined a slight that did not occur. After all, Miss Krupp was a nice person who just happened to teach Spanish. She wouldn't shoot him down because of an unfounded — and rapidly spread — rumor that he was linked to French royalty. Or would she?

Lewis may have been unclear about Miss Krupp's opinion of the rumor, yet there was no doubting Mr. Mueller's take on the matter in second-period history. The man was lecturing the class on English history when he paused, peered at Lewis with amusement, and said, "Perhaps our contender for the French crown can tell us what year the Magna Carta was issued."

Although Lewis, realizing Mr. Mueller was joking, had known to reply, "Twelve-fifteen," giving the correct answer did nothing to diminish the intense mortification he felt at that moment.

The situation went from bad to worse. While walking in the hallway to his third-period class, a gaggle of freshmen girls whom Lewis hardly knew blushed and giggled when they saw him. He frowned at the lot, only to hear one of the girls exclaim, "Did you see that?! His Excellency noticed me. Praise the Lord."

By the time lunch break rolled around, Lewis was beginning to think the situation could deteriorate no further, but when he walked into the cafeteria, everyone present — cooks, hall monitors, and janitors included

— fell silent and watched him as he trudged through the food line with his tray. Lewis glanced out at the sea of faces and was horrified to see what appeared to be a plethora of reverent expressions. He wanted to scream and run. Instead, he carried his tray to an empty table in the corner of the room and sat with his head bent over his food.

Lewis heard a chair scrape the floor and looked up. He clenched his jaw and glared at Amanda as she sat. She met his angry gaze with an innocent look, and he snarled, "I should have known better than to share any personal matters with you."

"What?"

"You know what. Someone intentionally spread a rumor all around school that I'm the descendant of a French king, and I'm looking at that someone now."

Amanda's expression darkened. "You've jumped to the wrong conclusion, Lewis. I did nothing intentional."

"I find that hard to believe."

"Well, it's true. What happened was, yesterday after you left Chip's, some other friends showed up and we were all talking, and Misty and I must have mentioned the conversation we'd just had with you. So maybe I am responsible for the news getting out, but that's not the same as intentionally spreading a rumor."

Lewis was mum. How could he possibly respond to such lawyerly rationale?

"If you want to apologize to me," Amanda cooed, "I'll accept."

"You'll accept?" Lewis was incredulous. "It's my life that's being turned upside down here. Did my feelings ever cross your mind? I mean, how am I supposed to react to all this?"

"You could start by calming down."

"What are you, insane?"

"No. But funny you should ask, since you're the one who's acting crazy. Of course I realize this might be difficult for you at a time when you're trying to decide whether to search for your mother."

"I'm not wondering any such thing. And quit trying to change the subject."

"It seems to me the same subject," Amanda countered. "If you found your mother and she knew who her parents were — which she probably does — you'd be two steps closer to knowing whether your blood is blue or not."

"Sounds as if you already take it as fact," said Lewis.

"Why not? I mean, even if it isn't true, what's the harm in a few people thinking you have a spot of royal blood? Slippery Falls is a boring, old ladder-factory town. We never get any real excitement here. Let the public have a little fun."

Lewis sighed and said nothing. As was often the case when conversing with Amanda Dot, he was feeling utterly exasperated.

ELEVEN

Lewis grew gloomier and gloomier as the school day wore on. By the time the final bell rang, he was feeling so downtrodden and dispirited, he could not imagine ever being cheerful or optimistic again.

The next day brought more of the same, and it took an effort of will for Lewis to hold his head up as he walked through the hallways between classes. "Make way for His Majesty" and "Long live the king" were the most popular cheers, with "All hail the illustrious monarch" coming in a close third.

Somehow, hour by tedious hour, Lewis made it through all six periods on Friday without suffering a breathing fit or otherwise falling apart. He slunk to the park after school, where he sat on a bench listening to Slippery Falls ask, *Whooorrruu? Whooorrruu?*

The *biggest joke in Idaho* was Lewis's internal answer.

He'd been hunched over with his head in his hands for a dour length of time when he chanced to look up and see Sophie Joilet on a bench fifty yards away. She held a book in her hands. He watched her read for a few moments, then got up and walked over. "Hi, Sophie. Hope I'm not interrupting."

Sophie closed the book and smiled.

"Does Catherine the Great tell a good story?" Lewis asked as he sat down beside her.

"She had an interesting life, that's for sure. I don't know if I'd call her story good. She was kind of wild, actually."

"Oh," said Lewis, turning to stare at the waterfall.

"You've had a rough week, haven't you?"

"Yeah." Lewis drew a breath and heaved a resigned sigh. "The worst of it may be over, though. The ridicule was a little less today than yesterday. That's promising."

"Sometimes I think people are idiots," Sophie said with a flash of anger. "Most of them never stop to think about anyone's feelings but their own."

Surprised by the outburst, Lewis turned from the waterfall and studied Sophie anew. He saw a certain feisty allure that he'd never noticed before. It jostled his spirits and prompted him to quip, "You French girls have pluck."

Sophie scowled facetiously.

Lewis grinned and relaxed. "So Sophie, just curious. When you listen to the waterfall, what do you hear?"

Sophie looked perplexed.

"Does the waterfall say anything to you?" Lewis clarified.

Seeing that Lewis was serious, Sophie turned toward the gorge and concentrated. Seconds later, she nodded and said triumphantly, "I hear it now. It says, *You are you.*"

Lewis was flummoxed. "Really?! That's what you hear?"

"Yes. Listen. It's saying, *Youurrruu. Youurruu.*"

Lewis jumped to his feet. "Perfect."

"What's perfect?" wondered Sophie.

"What the waterfall says. I've been thinking it said, *Who are you?* Obviously I was wrong, and it took you to tell me. Thank you, Sophie. Thank you, thank you."

Sophie was wary. She could not determine if Lewis was teasing her. Her doubt dissolved when he said, "Come on. Let's hit Chip's and I'll buy you a milk shake."

"Sounds like a plan." Sophie picked up her book and popped to her feet.

As plans go, there were no intrinsic flaws in the idea of heading to Chip's for a milk shake. Yet as the pair was about to discover, an unforeseeable snag existed. The snag was spelled out on a sign that hung on the front door.

CHIP'S COFFEE SHOP IS NOW CHIP'S CAFÉ

SERVING FRENCH FRIES AND SOUP DU JOUR
WITH CROUTONS FROM SEVEN TO NINE,

Lewis staggered on the sidewalk.

"C'est fou," Sophie swore, then, seeing the devastation on Lewis's face, offered, "I understand if you don't want to go in."

"I don't. Not now. Maybe some other time."

Sophie acquiesced with a look and accompanied Lewis as he walked away. They'd not gone far when he asked, "What did you say just now in French?"

"I said, 'It's crazy.' I meant life."

Lewis nodded. He couldn't agree more.

The next morning Lewis collected the books off the night table and headed to Maple's house. He had reached the end of his rope with all the royal flapdoodle and — for the moment, at least — wished to separate himself from all things French.

He passed through the gate and was approaching the front door of Maple's house when it swung open and Itsy Powers stepped out. A woman with a nose for everybody's business, she gazed knowingly at Lewis and said, "La-di-da. There you are, the talk of the town."

Lewis grimaced. "Hello, Mrs. Powers."

"I'm not expected to bow down, am I, Sire?"

"No, ma'am," Lewis said in a sinking voice. "All that talk is nonsense, Mrs. Powers. It wasn't me who spread the rumor. I'm the same, ordinary Lewis Hinton I always was."

Itsy looked disappointed. "What are you, a pooper?"

"Excuse me?"

"Someone has to play the goat," Itsy replied. "Don't you know all societies need a foil to stay healthy?"

"Yes, ma'am. I mean, no, ma'am," Lewis stammered. "I've never thought much about goats."

"Well, you should start now, seeing as everyone already thinks you're special."

"But I'm not."

"No?" Itsy frowned. "Why not?"

"I, ah . . . I'm just an ordinary guy, Mrs. Powers."

Itsy snorted and brushed past Lewis. "You modern-day youngsters. There's no drama in your blood. Not an ounce of pizzazz to divide amongst you."

A flabbergasted Lewis was watching the little white-haired dynamo bounce down Main Street when he heard Maple call from an upstairs window, "Don't just stand there, Lewis. Come on in."

Upon entering the foyer and hearing a step creak, Lewis looked up and saw Maple on an upper landing in a bright purple jumpsuit.

She saw his shock and inquired, "What do you think?"

Lewis hesitated. "Nice color. Very unusual."

"Thank you." Maple proudly descended the stairs. "It's hot violet. I made it myself, of course."

"It's nice," Lewis managed to reply.

"Glad you approve," Maple trilled. "I suspect you're wondering what came over me. Well, I was having a bath last night when it struck me that I've been wearing the same old dresses since I met Wickham, and — call it an inspired change — I decided it was time for a new look."

Lewis felt suddenly remiss. He'd been so caught up in his own dilemmas, he had not paused to recall that Wickham had given up the ghost almost exactly a year ago. "It's a stunning outfit. I'm sure Mr. Baderhoovenlisterah would have liked it."

Maple paused in the thought, then changed

the subject. "Itsy tells me tongues have been wagging about you, Lewis. She said it's all over that you are the great-great-great-great-great-great-great-grandson of a French king."

"It's true," Lewis confirmed. "And it's driving me mad."

"Come," said Maple, taking the books from Lewis and carrying them to the library. After returning them to their proper shelves, she hemmed and said, "So, the whole town has latched on to your story. I guess everyone has a little plausibility stretching in their blood."

Lewis stared off into space, a faraway look in his eye.

"Something I can help you with?" asked Maple.

"Yes," said Lewis. "I understand the concept of telling a story with one's life, but what I'm not sure of is, why?"

Maple's eyes twinkled with delight. She loved answering esoteric questions. "When you tell a story, you have to describe its parts and link them in meaningful ways, and to do that, you must observe and understand those parts in a larger context. That calls for concentrated thinking, which is why one ought to tell a story with their life. Concentrated thinking — it's a tried-and-true, good, old-fashioned habit."

"Makes sense to me," Lewis allowed after a moment's reflection. "So, you're saying that telling a story with your life is basically a matter of observing and understanding and thinking."

"Couldn't have put it better myself," noted Maple. "There is, however, an additional element to consider. It's called participation. Life, with all its constant changes, is similar to a river, Lewis, and sometimes you have to get in your boat and row. Otherwise you spin around in eddies and drift randomly on crosscurrents."

Lewis bobbed his head in comprehension and said, "In that case, I guess once you start telling your story, the process goes on forever."

Maple concurred, "If you can concentrate that long, it does."

TWELVE

Lewis awoke on Sunday with the voice of Itsy Powers in his head. "Someone has to play the goat." Although he abstractly understood what she'd been saying, her words did not take on concrete meaning until a short while later, when Mayor Greenly followed Martha and Avery home from church. The mayor and Lewis's parents found him lounging on the back patio. "Constance wishes to speak with you about some civic matter, son," Martha announced in an obviously vexed tone. "I don't know what it's about, as she won't tell your father or me."

Constance looked contritely at Martha, as if to say, *Don't you trust your mayor?*, then turned to Lewis. "I'll come straight to the point, Lewis. I'd like to feature you on the Welcome to Slippery Falls Web site I'm developing. I want to spotlight you in 'Our Outstanding Citizens' section."

Lewis got to his feet and did some quick

thinking. He knew what motivated the mayor, yet did not know if Martha and Avery were aware of the gossip about him. He assumed they'd probably heard something, but — since they'd not said anything to him — held out hope that they were unaware of the rumor. At any rate, Lewis did not wish to discuss the matter in their presence, and told the mayor, "I'm honored to be asked, Mayor Greenly, but if you don't mind, I'd like to consider a few days before deciding."

This was not the reply Mayor Constance Greenly had wished to hear; however — given the skeptical stare Martha was shooting her way and her own shrewd instincts for political survival — she was effectively compelled to accede, "Of course you may consider before deciding to accept, Lewis. My store is open six days a week. You know where to find me."

Lewis dipped his head and took a step backward, relieved that the conversation had ended. If Martha and Avery were to hear he was possibly descended from a king, he wanted to be the one who told them . . . and if they'd already heard . . . well, he'd discuss it with them when they brought up the subject.

Mayor Greenly was hardly out of the house before Lewis realized what he had to do. As Maple had said, "Sometimes you have to get in your boat and row."

He dialed Amanda Dot's number, and she answered on the second ring. Lewis said hello and asked, "Would you meet me in the park in twenty minutes? I need to discuss something with you. It's important."

Amanda deliberated briefly before replying, "I was supposed to get a moped driving lesson from Gaston at two-thirty, but seeing as it's important, I'll call Gaston and have him pick me up in the park."

Grrrr, thought Lewis as he hung up the phone. *Why don't Amanda and Gaston just come out and admit they are a couple? Why do they even bother to pretend otherwise?*

Lewis was waiting on the bench closest to the waterfall when Amanda arrived. "So what's on your mind?" She sat next to him and, before he could reply, quickly added, "What's on your lip? Are you growing a mustache?"

"I've been thinking I might grow one."

Amanda had no need for thinking. "It's your prerogative, Lewis, but if you want my opinion, DON'T. You have a handsome face as it is. Please, spare your friends the mustache."

Lewis looked sheepish.

"Was that the important thing you wanted to talk about?"

"No." Lewis sat up straight. "I want to discuss the rumor about me being related to King Louis the Fifteenth. It's gotten way out of hand. Mayor Greenly was at the house not half an hour ago trying to enlist me in her tourist-development plans. She wants to put me on the town Web site and use me to attract tourists."

"She's a real go-getter, that woman."

"AMANDA."

"What?"

"I don't want my name and picture on a Web site. In fact, the reason I called you is I need your help squelching all this crazy talk about me and Madame de Pompadour."

"How do you propose to do that?"

"By speaking to you," Lewis replied pithily. "You got the rumor started. You figure out how to stop it."

Amanda said with a gaze that she did not appreciate Lewis's tone, then paused in strategic thought and soon proclaimed, "It's easy. I'll tell everyone we researched the matter and discovered you're actually descended from a peasant. And to be on the safe side, I'll add that anyone mentioning the matter in public again will personally bear the brunt of my wrath." Amanda batted her eyelashes and looked innocently at Lewis. "How's that?"

Lewis could not refrain from smiling. "I

knew I could count on you, Amanda. You're a genius."

"Thanks. I was beginning to think you'd never notice."

"Oh, there's plenty that I've noticed about you," Lewis offered sincerely.

"Oh? Like what?" Amanda batted her eyelashes again.

But Lewis did not reply, for the delicate moment was abruptly terminated by the high-pitched whining of a two-stroke engine. It was Gaston, zooming across the park on his moped.

The next morning before dressing and heading to school, Lewis put a new blade in his razor and shaved all the golden fuzz from his cheeks, chin, and upper lip.

His arrival at Slippery Falls High was heralded by a cluster of freshmen who bowed and curtsied as he walked up the front steps. It was, Lewis feared, going to be another tedious day of unwanted attention. But as the morning unfolded, it became clear to Lewis that the ninth graders on the front steps had yet to hear of Amanda Dot's latest edict, which was still being circulated through the student body. Later in the lunchroom, when Lewis saw the offending freshmen, they pretended as if they did not notice him. By this point there had been a radical change in the public's conduct toward Lewis. The change, he knew, stood in shining testament to the social acumen and clout of Amanda Dot.

When the treat-Lewis-as-a-normal-person trend carried over into Tuesday and Wednesday, then remained in force on Thursday, a proverbial weight was lifted from his shoulders. Suddenly, Lewis felt free to relax about who he was or might be, and resume composing his own story. Ironically, perhaps, the less interested the public was in Lewis's royal ancestry, the more he was inclined to hypothesize and muse on the subject. Blue blood aside, he was pretty certain he was French, which is why he asked Sophie Joilet to meet him at Chip's on Friday afternoon.

The café sign had been removed and the place was called Chip's Coffee Shop again. Lewis arrived first and secured the front booth, and when Sophie joined him, he told her, "I have something to ask you. Feel free to say no if you want. I'll understand."

She eyed Lewis curiously and waited.

"Would you teach me to speak French?"

The curious look on Sophie's face was replaced by a gravely reserved expression.

"Never mind," said Lewis. "I see you're not interested."

The lines in Sophie's face softened. "What you see is not unwillingness, Lewis. It's the language that worries me. I grew up with it, so it comes naturally to me, but learning to speak proper French is not easily done. It takes a real commitment . . . as well as a finely tuned ear."

"My hearing is fine."

"Oh? Like at the waterfall?"

"That doesn't count," Lewis responded defensively, then had second thoughts. "Does it?"

Sophie laughed. "No, the waterfall doesn't count, although you may wish it did after your first few French lessons."

"Is that a yes?"

"Oui, Lewis. It's a yes."

"Great. When do we begin?"

"Tomorrow, if you wish. Let's meet in the park. Say one o'clock? We could make Saturday our regular day for lessons."

"That's great, Sophie. Thanks a lot. I'll be there with my ears, rain or shine."

Sophie smiled dubiously. She knew better than Lewis the frustrations he was about to encounter.

And thus, the following day, Lewis began to learn to speak what he believed to be the language of his ancestors. It was slow going that first Saturday, and slow going the following week, and had all the earmarks of being slow going for many months to come. Still, Lewis's desire to learn his native tongue was strong, and he persisted. His patient instructor, Sophie, endured.

In the days and weeks between each lesson, the Little Lost River continued pouring from its high plateau, the stars shifted their positions in the sky, and the school year mercifully marched to a close. The blessed summer season soon arrived in Idaho, and kids all across the state got busy having fun. For Lewis — who spent most of his days on his sitting rock, fishing for the elusive trout in the hidden pool — the appearance of summer meant the date was approaching when he would cross the gorge, lay down a ladder bridge, and venture into the uncharted cavern behind Slippery Falls.

THiRTEEN

On the first rainy day in June, which fell in the middle of the month, Lewis walked into Greenly's Variety Store and told the mayor he did not wish to be featured on her Welcome to Slippery Falls Web site. To his relief, she replied, "It's not a problem. I'm on to something else hot. In fact, I'm waiting for the Travel Channel to answer the letter I sent last week. By the way, just for curiosity's sake, are you related to Madame de Pompadour?"

"To be honest, Mrs. Greenly — I mean, Mayor — I don't know."

"Hmm. Well. Have a nice day."

"I will, if it ever stops raining."

Lewis had recently given a lot of thought to Amanda's repeated exhortations that he search for his biological mother, and as he sloshed home from Greenly's Variety Store he boldly decided to bring the matter up with

Martha. He found her reading in the living room and said, "Mom, may I ask you a hypothetical question?"

"Of course, son." Martha closed and put away her magazine. "You know you can ask me anything."

Lewis braced himself with a deep breath. "Let's suppose, in theory, that maybe I wanted to try to find my birth mother. How would you feel about that?"

"Is that what you've decided to do?"

"No. It's a hypothetical question. I was just wondering how you'd feel if I should decide to search for her."

Martha made a noise that was part hem and part moan. "I've been expecting something like this since people started saying you might be kin to a French king."

"You heard about that?"

"Of course I heard. It's not possible for everyone in Slippery Falls to gossip about a matter and me not hear of it eventually. I appreciate that you never brought the subject up at home."

"I didn't think it was worth mentioning, seeing as there is no proof that it's true."

Martha sighed and looked down at her hands. Then, after a moment, she raised her gaze and allowed, "I suppose it's only fair that I answer your question."

Lewis assumed a neutral expression.

"I would understand if you chose to look for your birth mother," Martha said softly, a little sadly. "Yet to be honest with you, I don't know how I would feel. A part of me would be afraid . . . for you and what you might find . . . and for Avery and me, and what we might lose."

Lewis felt a lump rise in his throat. "You wouldn't lose anything, Mom. We're family. If I searched for J. A. Poisson, and if by chance I found her, she would be a stranger I was meeting for the first time. I'd still be your son, Lewis Hinton. That will never change."

The lump in Lewis's throat was an

insignificant mass compared with the swelling that now clogged Martha's esophagus. She gulped, repressed a sob, and said, "That was beautifully spoken, Lewis. I doubt if Danielle Steele could've written anything more perfect for you to tell me just now. You should try writing stories. You might be good at that."

"Maybe." Lewis chuckled quietly.

Martha cleared her throat and said in an overtly relieved tone of voice, "Now that you've successfully reassured anxious old me, I can say that if you decide to go searching for your other mother, you will have my blessing. And Avery's, too. I can vouch for him."

"Thanks, Mom. You're a saint."

"Yes. Well . . . just keep me apprised of your plans."

Although the big fish did not bite and Lewis's tongue persisted in obstinately rebelling against the French language, his personal story moved along rather smoothly until the thirtieth of June.

He was in the park with Sophie, receiving his sixth French lesson, when she puckered her lips to show him the correct way to enunciate l'*amour* and he — succumbing to a rogue urge that appeared out of nowhere — leaned over to kiss his tutor's lips.

Sophie drew back swiftly. Although she did not raise a hand to slap Lewis, she appeared as though she might.

He shrank into himself and whimpered, "I'm sorry. I don't know what I was thinking."

Sophie glared at Lewis with impassive disapproval.

He looked at the ground and moaned. "I'm such an idiot."

A long twenty seconds passed before Sophie said, "It's done now. Forget it, Lewis. Just don't surprise me like that again."

Lewis did not look up. "No. Never."

"I believe that's enough French for today. Study your vocabulary during the week and we'll pick up where we left off next Saturday."

Lewis continued staring at the ground for several sullen minutes after Sophie departed. He could not shake the feeling that he'd done something irrevocably wrong, nor comprehend why. Was it his French blood? Had a genetic impulse goaded him to kiss his friend Sophie? Granted, she was cute, but she was not the girl in his heart.

Lewis rose heavily to his feet. He caught a movement of color in the right corner of his eye and turned. Some fifty yards to the south, Amanda Dot and Misty Dean were walking away from the fence by the cliffs, heading out of the park. Lewis cringed and waited, and wondered how long they'd been by the fence . . . and what they had seen. The pair proceeded from the park without so much as half a glance in his direction. It seemed to him as if Amanda and Misty had been walking fast, intentionally not looking in his direction.

Lewis could not bear to contemplate what may or may not have just happened. In fact, he was so anxious to forget the experience, he leaped to a decision that had nothing to do with trying to kiss Sophie or what Amanda might have seen. The decision drove him home, where he picked up the phone and called Gaston.

"Yellow."

"Gaston. It's me, Lewis."

"That's a surprise. What's up?"

"I have a favor to ask. You don't owe me one or anything."

"I'm open-minded. What do you need?"

Lewis described the ladder he was seeking and said he was hoping to borrow one for a day.

"Sounds like a Vermont Apple Picker to me," observed Gaston. "I can check the factory inventory on our home computer and see if we have any fourteen-footers in stock. Mind telling me why you want it?"

"It's not something I want to discuss on the phone. It's sort of a secret. Actually, I was thinking of asking you for help with what I'm planning."

"Hmph. Let me see what I find and then we'll talk. I could meet you at Chip's later."

"That's good," said Lewis. "Eight o'clock?"

"Sure thing."

That night, Lewis and Gaston sat in a back booth and Gaston reported, "There're five Apple Pickers in stock, all fourteen-footers. Shouldn't be a problem borrowing one. It'll have to be an unofficial loan, of course. I have keys to both warehouses, but I'm not supposed to take stuff out."

"I don't want to get you in any trouble."

"Very gentlemanly of you. Tell you what. You explain what you're up to, and I'll decide if it's worth my while."

Lewis reminded Gaston of the big fish he'd been trying to catch, told of discovering the cavern, and laid out his plan.

Gaston peered skeptically at Lewis. "You serious?"

Lewis nodded. "Dead serious."

Gaston snorted. "From the sound of it, you might wind up seriously dead."

"You know I have a lot of climbing experience. I wouldn't do this if I didn't think it would work."

Gaston saw determination in Lewis's eyes and said, "You sold me. When do you need the ladder?"

"I'm ready now. When can we get it?"

Gaston considered a moment. "Tomorrow after dark. It's Sunday, and the factory is closed all next week for Fourth of July. I could take Mom's station wagon and we could sneak it across the bridge."

"Perfect. I'll meet you here this time tomorrow."

Gaston agreed to the rendezvous, then said, "Now I have a question. Did you and Amanda have a fight or something?"

"Where'd you get that idea?"

"From Amanda. She called before I came

to meet you, and when I suggested she meet us here at eight-thirty, she said she wasn't interested in seeing Lewis Hinton tonight. She sounded mad."

Lewis's chest grew tight.

Gaston shrugged. "It's probably nothing. You know how girls can be."

FOURTEEN

Just after twilight on Sunday, July first, Gaston and Lewis filched a fourteen-foot Vermont Apple Picker from the Slippery Falls Footstool and Ladder Factory and drove it over the bridge in Gloria Fullup's station wagon. They stashed the "borrowed item" in the woods near the road and agreed to meet at the spot at ten-thirty the next day.

The next morning Lewis gobbled a quick breakfast and entered the garage, where he produced a fishing rig short enough to be carried through the confines of the cavern. From butt to tip, the pole stood eighteen inches tall. He was about to depart for his appointment with Gaston when, on a lark, he went into his bedroom and grabbed the maroon beret off the back of the chair, where it had hung now for more than a month.

Arriving at the bridge, Lewis saw Turly, Hank, and Tom leaning over the rail. When

Turly saw Lewis, he erupted with laughter. "Well, lookey there! It's the French king, carrying a toddler's pole."

"I reckon he'll reign them in now," cackled Hank. "Reign. Get it?"

Tom smiled broadly and nodded.

"Good day, gentlemen," Lewis said as he marched by. He didn't have time to stop and chat with a bunch of doubting old men.

Lewis entered the woods beyond the bridge, dragged the ladder from its hiding spot onto the path, and sat down to wait. Some fifteen minutes later, he heard the sound of a moped. Gaston arrived and stuck his bike in a thicket. Then — after no more than a hello between them — the pair picked up the Vermont Apple Picker and started toward the bluffs on the east side of the gorge.

As they drew closer to their goal and Gaston got a good look at the mound of boulders by the raging waterfall, he was compelled to wonder, "Lewis, do you honestly think this will work?"

"I do."

"And the cavern behind the falls, what do you know about it?"

"I know it's there."

Gaston halted, and since they were carrying the same ladder, Lewis halted as well. When Lewis turned around, Gaston inquired, "Have you lost your mind?"

"Not that I'm aware of," Lewis replied with a touch of annoyance in his voice. "Listen, Gaston. I know what I'm planning is tricky, and that if worse comes to worst, I could get hurt. I knew it when I had the idea, and have known it ever since. Even so, I'm here to accomplish something that's important to me, and I'm going for it, with or without your help. The fact is, you've already done more than I had a right to expect. You got me the ladder. I'll understand if you want to turn around and go home."

Gaston chortled. "It's cool, man. I just

asked if you'd lost your mind. I've come this far. I'm not going to back out now."

"Good," said Lewis, turning and preparing to march.

"Hup," Gaston entreated. "Just a second."

"What now?"

"Something I've been wondering, Lewis. This fish you're after. No one else has seen it. Are you sure it exists?"

Lewis paused to reflect, then told Gaston, "I believe it exists. About a year ago, I was on the cliffs and the wind was blowing pretty hard, and the falls suddenly split apart, for just a couple of seconds. When it opened I saw a pool of water behind the falls . . . and there was a shadow of a huge fish in the pool."

"That's it? That's all you're going on?"

"Yep," Lewis said plainly. "One glimpse. That's what I'm going on."

Gaston grinned with admiration and

amusement, and exerted forward pressure on the ladder. "Lead on."

It took some derring-do and fussing, yet they soon reached the penultimate boulder and hoisted the Apple Picker broadside onto the pinnacle. Lewis climbed up with his fishing rod and raised the ladder erect. Gaston followed, and although it was apparent from the look on his face that he was not comfortable standing on the elevated, round stone surface, he suppressed his trepidation and asked, "Now what?"

Lewis explained. "Basically, we tilt the ladder slowly down toward the cavern. I'll try to guide the tip so it catches the opening, while you keep your weight on the bottom rung."

"So I'm just an anchor, right?"

"You'll be more than just the anchor when I crawl out on the ladder," Lewis corrected. "You'll be The Great Important

Anchor That Keeps the Bridge from Flipping and Me from Falling."

They both looked down, and Gaston observed, "It's a lot of responsibility, being an anchor."

"You'll do fine. Just don't let go, no matter what happens."

"Right," Gaston whispered.

"Slowly now," said Lewis, and the pair began to let the narrow end of the ladder descend toward the waterfall. When the water hit the aluminum rails, the jerry-rigged bridge rattled violently and was forced abruptly down. Before they could react, the tip of the span caught the bottom lip of the cavern opening. "Bingo," cried Lewis. "Now Gaston, sit on the base and keep it stable while I crawl through the waterfall."

"I'll do my best."

Without further ado, Lewis clenched the fishing rod in one hand and crept out over the gorge. He was three-quarters of the way between the boulders and the falls when the ladder tilted laterally to the left. Gaston screamed and struggled to keep his end flat. Lewis scooted through the curtain of cold water and hooked his arms over the interior lip of the opening. The beret had been swept from his head, he was chilled and soaking wet, but he had a solid grip on the opening and everything was going more or less according to plan . . . until Lewis pulled himself forward, shifted his weight onto the lip of the cavern, and the ladder shot sideways from under him.

Lewis felt his legs lose contact with the Apple Picker, but did not see it swing out over the gorge, nor witness Gaston's heroic attempt to keep it from falling. Nor could Lewis clearly hear the swear that escaped from Gaston: "#*%!"

"WHAT?" hollered Lewis.

"I lost the . . . never mind, you're alive."

"I can't hear a word you're saying."

"What?" Gaston bellowed.

"I'm in," called Lewis, who was beginning to realize that the crevice that he'd optimistically referred to as a cavern was actually a dark, wet, steeply sloped, clay-lined trench. The only remotely encouraging feature he could discern about the trench was that it fell vaguely westward, where he was now committed to going.

He hesitated for a moment, and then — with the philosophical resignation that only a cold, wet person dangling from the lip of a trench behind a waterfall could know — slid forward, released his fishing rod, and dropped into the slippery chute.

He clawed at the clay and tried to slow his descent. He might as well have flapped his arms and attempted to fly, for he zipped ineluctably downward through the channel like a stone dropping from a tower. *BAM*. He careened over a muddy hump and flew through the air . . . and splashed backside-first into a basin of water.

He bobbed up like a cork and bumped into his fishing pole. He grabbed the pole and found his feet. The silvery curtain of Slippery Falls permitted enough light for him to see that he was in a three-sided, closet-sized chamber. An oblong window opened in the wall on the west side of the chamber. Lewis sloshed to the window, poked his head through the opening, and gazed into a much larger space. In the center of the space was a lagoon of still water.

Lewis could hardy believe his luck. He was staring at the coveted hidden pool!

Meanwhile, Tom Fitzboken was also marveling over his luck, for seconds earlier he had spotted a swatch of maroon fabric floating in the river and, with one masterful cast, had snagged the item, which he now realized was not a red salmon but a beret.

FiFTEEN

Lewis climbed through the opening and stood on a slender band of sand encircling the hidden pool. He knew it was unusual for a person to be where he was, doing what he was doing, yet at the same time the circumstances seemed strangely perfect to him. It was as if his entire life — or, certainly, the past year of it — had been leading up to this moment.

Lewis surveyed the space. Eight to ten feet above his head was an arched, earthen ceiling bespeckled with droplets of water. The walls of the cavern were made of igneous rock and densely packed clay. The cavern — and this was indeed a cavern — was about the size of an average school classroom. To Lewis's left, between him and Slippery Falls, was a six-foot-wide shelf of rock. Water sloshed back and forth from the river and pool through a shallow trough etched in the rock. Looking up and to the west, Lewis saw the underside of his sitting rock . . . and suddenly grasped the virtual impossibility of casting a lure from his perch into the pool. All this time, his silver spoon had never come close to the hidden pool.

He dropped to his knees and laid his rod on the sand. Spooked by his appearance, several minnows darted into the depths of the pool. He leaned forward and saw half a dozen mayfly nymphs wriggling in the water. A crayfish shot from the edge of the pool. Lewis was watching it recede when he saw a fish larger than the one he'd imagined.

He gasped. The creature hovered in the middle of the pool with its massive head above the surface. Two glassy eyes stared straight at Lewis, who felt as if he was in a dream . . . telling a fish story to beat all fish stories. Except Lewis was not in a dream, and he could not withdraw his gaze from the fish's intelligent, unwavering stare.

Suddenly, Lewis understood the how and

why of the trout's presence in the pool. It must have swum through the trough in the rock and entered the pool as a minnow, and feasted on mayfly nymphs. It had grown and graduated to crayfish, eventually swelling in size until it could no longer exit through the cut in the rock. From then on, the fish was a prisoner in the pool.

Poor old trout.

Moving slowly so as not to alarm the magnificent creature, Lewis waded into the pool. The trout appeared to understand his intent. It rotated lengthwise and positioned itself so Lewis could slip his arms under its belly. All this time, the great fish had been waiting for Lewis to come. Or so it seemed to Lewis, who would not have believed what was happening if he had not been there as a witness.

"Here we go, fellow," Lewis mumbled as he lifted the trout and held it to his chest. The great fish flapped its tail. It was happy.

Seven strides delivered Lewis and the trout

to the edge of the pool. Two more strides carried them across the strip of beach and onto the shelf of rock. One more stride took them halfway across the rock, where, unfortunately, a carpet of algae betrayed the weight of Lewis's foot and he flew in the air.

He was not aware of throwing the trout forward as he fell. It simply happened, just as he bounced off the rock without thinking and plunked into the agitated cauldron of churning river beneath the curtain of Slippery Falls.

An irresistible force thrust Lewis grave-deep under the surface and held him there for twenty seconds. It seemed much, much longer. The force dissipated, and Lewis felt himself rising. He did not rise far, for in the next instant a rip current grabbed him and swept him swiftly out into the gorge. He thought, I must go up for air. It was his last conscious thought before his head smacked against a rock and he was robbed of all ability to think.

Prior to this moment, a very distraught Gaston was still sitting on the mound of boulders where he'd last seen Lewis. Soon, over the roar of the falls, Gaston heard the faint sounds of a commotion in the distance and leaped to his feet. He looked south toward the bridge and saw two figures scrambling down a path that led to the river. It was Turly Sweed and Hank Maybe. Above them, on the bridge, Tom Fitzboken leaned over the rail and gesticulated wildly.

Gaston cupped his hands behind his ears and heard Tom shout, "The body is straight out, about fifty feet to your left."

Gaston descended the mound of boulders and ran along the high bluffs as fast as his feet would carry him. He grabbed his moped from the thicket, cranked the engine, and raced along the path through the woods and across the bridge. He dumped his bike in the road and sprang to Tom's side. Turly and Hank were waist-deep in the river, straining against the downstream current. Turly shouted, "He's floating faceup. There's hope yet."

"Hey, look!" cried Hank.

"What the . . . " Turly adjoined incredulously.

Then Gaston saw the source of their bewilderment. Lewis's body was cutting across the powerful flow of the river. Some unseen, unimaginable power was delivering it to his rescuers.

Sure enough, seconds later, Lewis floated straight into Turly's arms. Then Gaston saw the blood on Lewis's head and wondered, "Is he alive?"

Tom answered, "Must be. Dead people don't bleed like that."

As Turly carried Lewis toward the embankment beneath the bridge, he called to Gaston, "Get on your scooter and go tell Doc Riddle we're coming in with an emergency. Tell him we'll go to the back door of his office."

"And hurry," added Hank.

This last bit of instruction was unnecessary, as Gaston had already hopped on his moped and departed.

Amanda and Misty were on their way out of Chip's when Gaston zoomed by them on Main Street. They knew something was wrong when he failed to wave, much less stop and say hello. In an effort to see where he was heading in such a hurry, they stepped into the street. They watched him recede into the distance, then slide to a halt and throw down his bike outside of Doc Riddle's office.

"Somebody must be hurt," Amanda exclaimed.

"I hope not," Misty said in a sinking tone.

"Gaston sure was eager to get to Doc's."

"We should walk up and —" Misty's thought was cut short by the blast of a horn and the force of Amanda yanking her to the side. A nanosecond later, Hank Maybe's pickup truck blurred past. The girls returned immediately to their vantage point in the street. When they saw the pickup roar around to the back of Doc Riddle's office, Amanda turned to Misty with a shocked look on her face and said, "We'd better go find out what happened."

Misty started walking. "I hope no one we know got hurt."

Amanda groaned. "We know everyone in town."

Doc Riddle was a small man with a nervous twitch and more personal quirks than a jazz band. He abhorred small talk and rarely accepted social invitations in Slippery Falls. Nevertheless, he was an expert physician who could be relied upon in a medical crisis.

Doc was at the back door pulling on sterilized gloves when Turly lifted the bloodstained Lewis from the back of Hank's truck. Doc ushered Turly into the office, and together they laid Lewis on the bed. Doc began reading Lewis's pulse and said to Gaston, "Hand me a towel from the stack beside you. Put a couple others in the sink and run hot water on them."

Gaston — relieved to do something besides feel responsible for the situation — jumped to Doc's command.

Doc wiped the excess blood from Lewis's face and neck with the dry towel, then gestured to Gaston for a wet one. He used it to press gently on the gash now revealed on the top of Lewis's head. When the towel turned red, Doc threw it over his shoulder and bent to study the wound. He motioned for another towel and cleaned the wound again. Then, looking extremely dour, Doc said, "Someone go ask Martha Hinton what blood type Lewis has."

No one moved. Carrying bad news about Lewis to Martha was not a task anyone relished. While the bystanders were hesitating, Amanda and Misty appeared in the open back door. They took in the scene and went wide-eyed with horror.

Turly told the girls flatly, "He's alive. We need you to run and ask his mother what blood type he has."

"Yes, sir."

As Amanda and Misty whirled to leave, Doc called to them over his shoulder, "Say Lewis had a small accident and ask Martha to send dry clothes. Don't tell her what you saw here."

"No, sir."

Doc gave no further orders. He was busy snipping hair from Lewis's head, preparing the area around the wound for stitches.

It was three-fifteen when Avery answered a knock at the front door and found Amanda and Misty standing on the stoop. Martha could see the visitors from her seat in the kitchen. She welcomed them with a smile and a wave.

Avery was not smiling. He saw fright in Amanda's and Misty's eyes, and asked them point-blank, "What is it?"

"Lewis," Amanda said timidly.

"What about Lewis?" Avery wondered.

"A tiny accident," Misty peeped.

Avery called his wife.

"Coming," she replied crisply. She knew from his tone that the news was not good.

Amanda stepped bravely forward. "Mrs. Hinton, we need to find out what type of blood Lewis has."

"Who is 'we'?" Martha demanded.

"Doc Riddle wants to know. Lewis is in his office now."

Martha shot an alarmed look at Amanda. "How bad is he hurt?"

"I honestly don't know. We only saw him for a second or two, then Mr. Sweed sent us here to ask what his blood type was."

"He needs dry clothes, too," said Misty.

Martha had heard enough. "Avery, get the

car while I find Lewis's papers. Amanda, you know where Lewis's room is. Go fetch a change of clothes from his dresser."

Misty remained at the front door, watching Martha riffle through a desk in the living room. Martha located the manila envelope she was seeking and withdrew its contents. She found the paper she wanted and glanced at Misty, who blurted emotionally, "It's so terrible that this happened, Mrs. Hinton. It must be a huge shock for you."

Martha put the paper in her purse. "I've always known this day was coming."

SiXTEEN

Hank, Tom, and Turly were exiting Doc's office when Avery drove under the trees behind the building and parked by Hank's truck. The men nodded bleakly as the Hintons emerged from the car, then hung their heads in empathy as Martha gaped at Turly's bloody shirt. Amanda stepped from the rear of the car, took Martha by the arm, and led her into the building. Misty got out after Amanda and started to follow, then had second thoughts and decided to go find Lob and Sophie and tell them about Lewis. Avery stood looking at the three older men. "What happened?"

"There's been a miracle," Tom began. "Your boy lost a lot of blood, but he's holding on."

Solemn as a stone, Avery waited to hear more.

Words started gushing out of Turly. "We

were fishing like usual from the bridge when Tom said he saw something in the middle of the gorge and we all looked. It was a person floating, out where the current is strong. Didn't know then it was Lewis, but Hank and I rushed down to see what we could do. We didn't get far into the river before we had to stop or be swept away, which was what we thought was going to happen to Lewis . . . then the strangest thing happened."

"Very odd," mumbled Hank. "Looked as if something was holding him up in the water."

"It's true," Turly continued. "He cut across the river like he had a motor under his back."

"A motor?" Avery's voice was low and full of reservation.

"A motor of God, I'd say," offered Tom. "Something roiled under the water just as Turly got ahold of Lewis. It's beyond me to imagine, but it appeared to be a big fish."

"I saw it, too," adjoined Turly.

Avery looked doubtfully at the men. "I'm

not sure I follow what you're saying, but, well, I can't thank you enough for pulling Lewis out of the river."

Meanwhile, Martha had taken a pained look at Lewis and informed Doc Riddle that her boy was AB negative. Amanda was standing quietly in the corner beside Gaston. It would have been hard to measure which of the two teens felt worse.

Avery entered the room just as Martha was asking Doc, "Is there some problem with AB negative blood? Is it bad?"

"Not bad, but rare," Doc answered. "One in every hundred and sixty-seven people carry AB negative. Lewis would probably accept O negative. Turly has that and said it's ours if we ask; however, an exact match would be best. I'll call the Red Cross in Idaho Falls and have them send AB negative, but it takes awhile to get an order through, and" — Doc glanced at the clock — "it's twenty to four now. They might not deliver until tomorrow morning.

Lewis has lost a lot of blood, and his pressure is low. I'd rather he have a transfusion immediately."

Given the circumstances, Martha was bearing up commendably. However, the internal formulation of her next question put an obvious strain on her psyche. "Be straight with me, Doc. Will Lewis have brain damage?"

"I don't think so, yet I can't be certain without a brain scan." Doc paused, drew a long face, and peered at Martha. "Brain damage is the least of my concerns right now. He may not make it if we don't get his vitals up soon, and for that we need to give him blood."

Martha bit her bottom lip and thought hard. Seconds later she turned to Amanda and Gaston and said, "There are more than one hundred and sixty-seven people in Slippery Falls. You two go knocking on doors and find me someone with AB negative blood."

"Yes, ma'am," said Amanda.

"Right away," added Gaston.

Doc evidently endorsed the plan, because before the teens were out the door, he instructed, "Only healthy adults who know their blood type. I don't want well-meaning volunteers. No guessing."

"Got it," said Amanda.

"No guessing," Gaston repeated as he followed after Amanda.

Now there was just Martha and Avery watching Doc attend to their unconscious son, who barely seemed to breathe at all and clung to life by the thinnest of invisible threads.

Amanda and Gaston split up and began canvassing different sides of downtown Slippery Falls. Although neither of them met with early luck in locating an AB negative donor, they succeeded in quickly spreading the news about Lewis's condition. Thus when Amanda reached Maple Baderhoovenlisterah's address, the woman had already exited her house and was charging across the front yard. "I know why you're here," she told Amanda.

Amanda stepped back to avoid being hit by the gate.

"Might as well come with me," said Maple.

"I can't, Mrs. Baderhoovenlisterah. I'm on a mission."

"Consider it accomplished," Maple declared as she hurried down Main Street without pausing to see if Amanda followed or not.

The significance of Maple's remark had just begun to dawn on Amanda when she saw Sophie Joilet running toward her.

"I just heard." Sophie was panting as she came to a stop. "How is he?"

"Not good." Amanda's bottom lip trembled.

Sophie's eyes flooded with moisture. Then she and Amanda stepped simultaneously toward each other and embraced.

Back at Doc's office, Lewis's soiled clothes had been removed and a clean sheet had been placed over his body. The sheet now rose and fell slightly with each faint systole of his breath. He was otherwise as still and quiet as a winter night.

Doc Riddle was bent over the bed, scrutinizing the wound. The Hintons were standing behind him, praying wordlessly, when Maple burst through the door in tan pants and a cream-colored blouse. "I'm here," she announced, dipping her head in respectful concern to Martha and Avery.

"Hello, Maple," said Doc.

"Hi, Doc. Let's get started."

"Pardon me?"

"I'm AB negative."

"Oh." Doc was noticeably unmoved by the news.

Maple was not pleased with Doc's reaction. "What do you mean, 'oh'? The boy needs AB negative blood, does he not?"

"Yes, but you're too old to give blood. Sixty-five is the age limit. I might extend that a year or so, but not twenty."

"My blood is perkier than coffee, and you know it."

Doc stood his professional ground. "At your age, the bones are too brittle. They no longer contain enough marrow to produce ample blood for your own needs. You have no surplus to give away."

Maple huffed. "Listen, Doc. Lewis is in no position to wait for recommended ideals. I'm here with what he needs, so get your needle out and let's get started. Don't worry about me. I'll take iron and calcium supplements when I get home."

Doc balked and turned to Martha.

Martha looked at Doc, glanced quickly at Avery, turned, and met Maple's gaze. Ten intense seconds passed, then Martha told Doc, "I've known Maple all my life, and I know when she has a decided opinion on something, she's usually right. If you're looking to me for permission to use Maple's blood, I give it to you now."

Doc nodded at Martha and said to Maple, "Okay. But I'm only taking three hundred milliliters."

"Four hundred and fifty," Maple countered as she sat on the stool by the sink and pulled up her sleeve. "If he needs another pint later, we'll give him that, too."

As all this was going on, a small crowd had gathered under the trees outside of Doc's office and begun what would eventually become a town-wide vigil for Lewis. Although others were present as well, the crowd was centered around Amanda, Misty, Lob, Sophie, and Gaston. Everyone was helpless with nervous distress, and no one knew what to say or do . . . until Amanda suggested, "Let's hold hands in a circle and send Lewis our love."

Everyone did, of course.

SEVENTEEN

Doc kept a close check on Maple's eyes as he slowly withdrew blood from her arm. For all he could see, she remained stable, but that was because Maple artfully masked her distress. In fact, she had started to feel woozy after the first two hundred milliliters were taken and was growing progressively weaker with each passing second.

Her stomach stirred nauseously as blood hit the four hundred mark on the collection bag.

Maple's true condition was not revealed until after the final fifty milliliters of life-giving plasma were through the intake tube and Doc pulled the needle from her arm. He had wiped the needle clean and turned to place the blood bag on the counter when Maple closed her eyes and swooned sideways.

Avery, who was standing by Martha,

looking at Lewis, saw Maple falling and leaped to catch her before she hit the floor. Martha rushed to Avery's aid, and together they lowered the collapsed woman into a sitting position.

Doc reached into a cabinet for smelling salts, cracked open a vial, and waved it under Maple's nose.

The old woman's face twitched, her eyes blinked open, and she blurted, "I'm fine."

"Mercy," Martha trilled, and in a flush of relief told Maple, "I meant to mention this before, that's a lovely outfit you have on."

Maple sank weakly against Avery. "Thank you for noticing, Martha. I designed it myself."

Doc snorted derisively. For one thing, he knew Maple was not fine. For another, it seemed preposterous to speak of fashion at a moment like this. Doc squatted to study Maple. Seconds later he nodded toward an interior door and told Martha, "In my apartment there's orange juice in the fridge. Please get Maple a glass while I administer blood to Lewis." Doc glanced from Martha to Avery. "Holler if she faints again."

Maple struggled to sit up on her own power. "Who fainted? Not me. I just took a little nap."

"And you'll have plenty of big naps after I examine you," Doc retorted, "as you'll be confined to bed for at least a week."

"Horse droppings," Maple replied woozily.

Doc Riddle ignored his petulant patient and concentrated on infusing her donated blood into the unconscious one. Afterward, he checked Maple's vital signs and told Avery to call the Slippery Falls Volunteer Rescue Squad. "What do you need them for?" asked Maple. "You're a doctor."

"I am indeed," Doc answered flatly. "The rescue squad will be driving you home, Maple, where you will be staying in bed until I come around and say you can get up."

Later that afternoon the sun went behind a bank of low clouds, and the sky over Slippery Falls turned dull gray. At the same time, the air stopped moving and lay stagnant in the streets. All was silent except for the falling Little Lost. The mum populace was thinking of Lewis.

For many who had known Martha and Avery throughout their lives, Lewis represented the couple's salvation and was positive proof that the prayers of good people are answered.

For others, Lewis was a romantic hero, the closest they would ever come to knowing someone of royal descent.

For one brown-eyed singer, Lewis meant as much as anyone can mean for anyone. He was her best friend.

For two noble-hearted individuals, Lewis was the universe. He was their daily bread and coffee in the morning, their future and their son.

For three awed fishermen, Lewis was their

curious brethren who climbed in high places and was evidently blessed by the river beings.

For one medical practitioner, Lewis was a precarious patient who might revive or slip away at any instant.

For one bedridden woman, Lewis was the beloved recipient of the life-giving sauce that flowed through her veins.

For Lewis, there were no feelings or thoughts in his story. He was a chapter of blank pages.

A rumble of thunder punctuated the silence at twilight, and it began to rain after dark. The skies wept all night and did not cease until dawn the next morning.

At nine A.M. on that Tuesday, July third, the Red Cross delivery arrived from Idaho Falls. Doc, who along with the Hintons had been awake all night, gave Lewis a six hundred milliliter booster of blood, then went to take a nap. He was confident neither Martha nor Avery would let the boy go unwatched for a second.

Sure enough, when Doc later returned to the office at noon, the devoted couple was standing at the foot of the bed where he'd left them.

Unbeknownst to Doc or the Hintons, Mayor Constance Greenly had called an emergency meeting of the Slippery Falls Town Council for one o'clock sharp that afternoon. At issue was whether to postpone the annual Fourth of July fireworks, which were scheduled for the next evening. The prospect of holding a celebration (no matter how patriotic) while one of their own lay in jeopardy did not sit well with the council. After minimal debate, they voted five to zero to see how Lewis was doing at ten the next morning and make their decision then.

After the vote was recorded, Constance Greenly went to her variety store, grabbed a spool of purple ribbon from behind the counter, and walked the length of Main Street tying purple bows on benches, bicycles, flagpoles, signposts, and trees.

More than one person asked, "Why purple?"

And to each, the mayor replied, "Cleopatra's boat had purple sails. It's the imperial color of queens and kings."

At two o'clock that afternoon, Maple Baderhoovenlisterah was propped up in her bed when she heard a rap at her door. She knew who was rapping and replied somewhat curtly, "And what do you want now?"

The door opened, and Itsy Powers entered with a teapot and cup on a tray. "I thought you'd be wanting a spot of alfalfa tea about now."

"I told you an hour ago I didn't want tea."

"No, you didn't," Itsy corrected her friend. "I distinctly heard you say, 'Perhaps later.' And this is later, so don't get snippy with me."

"Sorry, Itsy. I suppose I'm not my usual self."

"Whatever 'usual' might be, I forgive you."

"Thank you." Maple gestured toward her night table. "You may set the tray here. I'll pour a cup later."

Itsy did as Maple suggested, then, before turning to leave the room, said, "Supper will be served early tonight. I'm making my famous egg-drop soup."

Maple rolled her eyes wearily. "I don't know what I did to deserve you."

"Nothing," Itsy said pointedly. "You're just lucky."

Lewis's status had not changed by six o'clock that evening. On several occasions earlier in the day, Doc had suggested to the Hintons that they might want to go home and eat and rest for a spell. However, each time he mentioned the idea, he was met with looks of resolute refusal.

Finally, that evening as the sun was

preparing to set over the Rocky Mountains, Doc went to the back door of his office, surveyed the group under the trees, and motioned for Amanda to approach. When she did, he said, "Don't tell me you've all been standing out here since yesterday."

"We haven't," Amanda answered. "Everyone went home last night. I returned at seven this morning. How is Lewis?"

The anxious crowd under the trees inched forward to better hear his reply. Aware of his audience, Doc answered loud enough for all to hear. "Lewis is holding steady, maybe improving a bit with each hour." A sigh of relief issued from under the trees, and Doc whispered to Amanda, "I need your help."

"Anything. What?"

"Come talk to the Hintons — see if you can convince them to go home and rest. I've been trying all day, but Martha won't listen, and Avery won't leave her side."

"I'll do my best," Amanda avowed before stepping past Doc into the office and going directly to Lewis's side. At a glance, he appeared much better than the last time she'd seen him. He had been washed of blood, and his stained shirt had been removed. Even so, "better" in this situation had limited value, for Lewis's head was wrapped in gauze, there was an IV tube in his arm, and he hardly seemed to breathe at all. She studied his slumbering face for nearly a minute, then turned purposefully and said to Martha, "He sleeps so sweetly. Doc thinks he's on the mend."

"We pray," Martha responded in an exhausted voice.

"I suppose after he wakes up and recovers he'll need a lot of watching."

Avery sensed what Amanda was attempting to achieve and added his support. "He'll no doubt be recuperating at home for weeks."

"I sure hope you'll call on me when the

time comes," Amanda continued to address Martha. "Looking after someone around the clock takes teamwork."

Martha knew what was going on . . . and understood that Amanda's campaign was well intentioned. She sighed and allowed, "Perhaps Avery and I could use a bite of food and a catnap. Amanda, if we went home for a spell, would you help Doc keep an eye on Lewis until we return?"

"Yes, ma'am. I'll watch him."

"And you'll let us know immediately if there's any change?"

"Right away."

"Thank you, dear. I'm glad Lewis has friends like you."

Amanda's heart tugged her three steps forward, and she gave Martha a quick embrace.

EiGHTEEN

Doc Riddle took Lewis's pulse after the Hintons departed and was pleased with the results. He then opened Lewis's mouth, saw a moist tongue, and decided to remove the IV feed from his arm. When that was done, he said to Amanda, "I'm in need of a shower and a short nap. Are you comfortable alone with Lewis if I step away for an hour?"

"I'll be okay," answered Amanda. "Do what you need to do, Doc. Don't worry about me."

Assured by Amanda's manner, Doc paused at his apartment door and adjusted the lights. "I'll leave these dim. The switch is here if you want the lights brighter. I might be a couple of hours. Don't hesitate to knock if there's any change in Lewis, or if you're in question about anything."

Amanda told Doc she wasn't the hesitating kind, and he left the room. She carried a metal stool to the side of Lewis's bed and sat down to cherish her imperiled friend. She'd been watching over him for approximately twenty minutes when she began to sing in a lush, lyrical voice.

"Someone is making
a puzzle of my heart.
Someone has caused the beating
to stop and start.
Speak to me."

Way off on the perimeter of the mirage where Lewis was drifting, he heard what sounded like an angel singing.

"You stand there within reach
so far, far away.
I can see
but cannot feel you."

The voice stirred deep in Lewis, and the mirage became a soothing oasis.

> "How can I ever know
> the colors of your glow
> when you hide inside
> standing there before me.
> I can love
> but cannot hear you
> speak to me."

Lewis's eyelids fluttered open. He did not know where he was or why, yet was warmed by the knowledge that he was somewhere with Amanda. "You sing so beautifully," he whispered.

Amanda gasped.

"You have a lovely voice."

Amanda trembled.

"That's a beautiful song," said Lewis. "What is it?"

" 'Speak to Me,' " Amanda answered, giddy with joy. "I wrote it a couple of months ago."

"It's great. I always thought you had talent. Now I know."

Amanda dropped to her feet and leaned over to look in Lewis's eyes. "You've come back."

"Back? From where?"

"I don't know. You were just gone."

Lewis scanned the room. "Where are we?"

"At Doc Riddle's. You've been unconscious since yesterday. You cracked your head on a rock in the river. Turly and his gang fished you out and brought you here. Gaston was with them."

Lewis reached up and touched the gauze bandage on his head. Slowly, the events of Monday came back to him.

Amanda could see that Lewis had begun to remember what happened before his arrival in Doc's office. She huffed and told him tersely, "You're a moron, Lewis. Gaston told me what you guys did. You could've killed yourself. Honestly! A lot of good that would have done."

Lewis grinned sheepishly. He was glad to

know Amanda had not changed during his lapse in consciousness.

She smirked affectionately at him and stepped back from the bed. "Excuse me while I wake Doc and call your parents. As you might imagine, Martha has been worried about you."

"Amanda."

"Yes?"

"Hold on a second. I want to tell you a couple of things." Amanda held, and Lewis said, "I just decided. I'm going to France."

"To look for your mother?"

"Maybe." Lewis paused and considered. "I might ask around to see if anyone knows her. Mostly, though, I want to see Paris and visit Versailles. That's where Madame de Pompadour and King Louis the Fifteenth lived. He was an orphan, you know."

"No, I didn't know that," Amanda said bleakly. She was less than thrilled about

Lewis's travel plan. "So what else? You said you had a couple of things to tell me."

Lewis struggled to rise up on an elbow. He desisted when Amanda ordered, "Don't move. Just lie there until Doc says don't lie there. I can hear you fine. Go ahead. I'm listening."

"I have a confession to make," Lewis ventured timorously. "It's sort of embarrassing. You might not know how I feel about you. I was going to say something that day when we spoke in the park, that day when Gaston gave you the moped lesson. Anyhow, Amanda . . . I think of you all the time."

A pregnant pause threatened to fill the room, then Amanda wondered, "Is that your confession?"

"No," Lewis said softly. "My confession is about Sophie. I, ah . . . I tried to kiss her. I'm not sure why. I don't have a crush on her or anything."

"I know. I saw you."

Lewis sank deeper into the bed and waited.

"I wasn't spying on you or anything. Misty and I just happened to be in the park admiring the waterfall, and you and Sophie were on a bench between us and the waterfall, so it was hard to miss it when you made your move."

"Oh."

Now it was Amanda's turn for confidential disclosures. "What I've never been able to understand, Lewis, is why you've never tried to kiss me."

"Because . . . well, I, ah . . . because of you and Gaston."

"What about me and Gaston?"

"You're a couple. Aren't you?"

Amanda made a noise that sounded like air escaping from a balloon. "Lewis, you've hit your head and lost a lot of blood, so I won't comment on your apparent lack of smarts. Gaston is gay, or thinks he might be. We are close friends. We're definitely not a couple."

"Gaston is gay?"

"He thinks so, and that's what counts for him. Of course, that's private news about Gaston. He's in the process of figuring himself out."

"I won't say a word."

"Good. This talk we're having will have to wait until you've recovered. I'm going now to wake Doc and call your mother."

Twelve minutes passed between the moment Martha received Amanda's call and the moment Avery stopped the car behind Doc Riddle's place. Doc heard the doors slam and stepped out to speak with the couple before they rushed inside. He wanted to inform them of Lewis's status and explain what he intended to do next. However, the only information Doc was initially able to impart came in response to Martha's rapid-fire questions. "He's awake?"

"Yes."

"And his mind's all there?"

"I believe so, based on a brief, superficial inspection. He's verbally cognitive."

"So what? You want to send him somewhere for tests?"

"Yes, Martha, I do. First thing tomorrow morning I want him in an ambulance on his way to Idaho Falls. Head injuries like his should be viewed by specialists with the proper equipment."

"Okay," Martha agreed. "So what's the bad news? You didn't step out here for fresh air."

"There is no bad news," Doc answered with a satisfied air. "I came out to remind you that Lewis has had a shock and ask you to remain calm when you see him. Don't ask too many questions and get him excited. I need him to rest."

"I'll be as calm as only a mother can be," Martha said as she took Avery's hand and proceeded into the office.

● ● ●

The ambulance picked up Lewis at seven-fifteen the next morning and, with Doc Riddle and Martha Hinton riding at his side, drove him to the hospital in Idaho Falls. Dr. Kinstry, the brain specialist attached to the hospital, was not tickled to be called in on an emergency on the Fourth of July. However, it didn't take her terribly long to run a few diagnostic tests on Lewis and render a professional conclusion. She found the Hintons in the waiting room. "Your son suffered a moderate concussion, but I'm glad to say that his skull was not fractured and he shows no signs of permanent injury."

"Any problems with his blood?" wondered Avery.

"None."

"No special treatments?" asked Martha.

Dr. Kinstry shook her head. "No, all he requires is several days' rest in bed. I trust Dr. Riddle to monitor the head wound and remove the stitches when they're ready to come out. He did a fine job of putting them there in the first place."

Martha was about to ask another question when a set of double doors swung open and Lewis appeared with Doc Riddle in the waiting room. At this point Martha forgot what she didn't know and was so happy, she didn't care.

NiNETEEN

Doc and the Hintons were back in Slippery Falls just after two o'clock that afternoon. Within an hour of their return, everyone in town knew Lewis was home and likely to fully recover. Mayor Greenly called her fellow council members on the telephone, and they voted unanimously to proceed with the fireworks display scheduled for later that evening. The council also okayed her motion that she use the occasion to deliver a speech in honor of the three local heroes who had saved Lewis.

Lewis was fed a hearty lunch and put to bed, and when an exhausted Martha and Avery retired to the master bedroom for a nap, Lewis was both alone and awake for the first time since his head smacked the rock in the river. He thought back to the evening he received his mother's letter, then recalled the consequential chain of events that had befallen him in the weeks that followed. So much had happened between the reading of the letter and the pair of glassy fish eyes staring at him from across the hidden pool, he had the impression he was recalling a movie or book about a boy named Lewis . . . and then it hit him: That's how one tells a story.

He laughed and mused: It's life. It's easy. You think about what you believe, jump in the river, and go with the flow. All you have to do is pay attention.

Now that Lewis had straightened out the larger philosophical picture of life, he began contemplating Amanda Dot. Amanda with the vivacious brown eyes and pretty, round face. Amanda who knew herself so well, she understood everyone else. Amanda who could sing like an angel. Amanda who was not dating Gaston.

Lewis fell asleep thinking of Amanda and dreamed about her until early that evening, when he was awakened by a knock at his bedroom door. "Yes?"

The door opened, and Martha peeked in the room. "I didn't want to disturb you, but you have a visitor."

"Send them in."

It was Gaston, whom Lewis had not seen since crawling over the gorge on the Apple Picker. They said hello and eyed each other with tentative reserve. Gaston took a seat in a chair by Lewis's bed, and offered, "Glad to see you're feeling better, Lewis. I'm sorry I blew it as your anchor. The ladder just got away from me. I couldn't help it."

"It fell, unh? I wasn't sure."

"Yeah."

"It's okay, Gaston. I got in the cavern."

"And then what happened?"

Lewis related his adventure in fair detail, beginning with a description of the trench and ending as he stepped through the wall and found the hidden pool.

"That's wild stuff. Did you see your big fish?"

Lewis was about to answer the question when some instinct bid him to hesitate. There was something almost sacred about his experience with the trout that made him reluctant to divulge all he knew. For reasons he could not articulate clearly to himself, he sensed that this part of the story would be best kept private, between him and the fish. "I saw it," he answered with a casual air, then added, "That was before I tried walking next to the waterfall. Stupid me, I slipped on wet rock and fell in the river right under the falls. Don't remember much after that."

Gaston had a hunch Lewis wasn't telling him everything, but he let it go and moved on to other matters. "So," he said with a light-hearted chuckle. "Amanda told me that you thought we were a couple. That's pretty funny, actually. I always saw you two as being cut out for each other."

"Hmph. I suppose it is funny."

"She say anything else?" Gaston feigned idle curiosity.

Lewis knew what was on Gaston's mind. "Naw. Not much. She called me a moron."

Gaston laughed and looked relieved.

"So . . . did you get the ladder back safely?"

"Nope. It belongs to the river now."

Lewis frowned. "I guess I should pay for it."

Gaston grinned. "That won't be necessary. I told Dad we took an Apple Picker and what happened, and he forgives us. He's big on voluntary confessions. He thinks they show character."

At this precise moment, less than a mile from Lewis's room, in Slippery Falls Park, Mayor Greenly concluded her veneration of the town's new heroes, and the first percussive boom of the annual fireworks show resounded in the skies above. Gaston took it as his cue, said good-bye to Lewis, and went to enjoy the show.

Moments later, Martha appeared at Lewis's

door with a cup of chicken broth. "Here, this should help you sleep, although no telling what your habits will be now that you have Maple's blood in your veins."

"Excuse me?!"

"Oh, you didn't know," Martha muttered.

"Didn't know what?"

Amidst a distant background of booming, hissing, whistling pyrotechnic discharges, Martha explained about Lewis's need for AB negative blood and how Maple had become his donor.

Lewis's first thought was: *I wonder if penchants are passed on in blood?* He expressed his second thought aloud. "She's old for giving blood, isn't she? Is she okay?"

"I hope so," said Martha. "Truth is, I've been so busy with you, I haven't heard. I know she was woozy when Doc sent her home to spend a week in bed."

"Oh." Lewis grew thoughtful.

Martha chose to leave him to his reflections

and said before going out the door, "Remember to drink your broth."

"Umhmm. I will."

Lewis was up and dressed by nine the next morning. Knowing he'd meet resistance from Martha, he found Avery in the kitchen and said, "Dad, I need a favor."

"What can I do for you?"

"Drive me to Mrs. Baderhoovenlisterah's house so I can tell her thanks for saving my life."

Avery furrowed his brow and stared uncertainly at Lewis. "Son, it's commendable that you want to express your gratitude to Maple. What she did was a good thing. But wouldn't it be better to wait a couple of days, give yourself a chance to finish mending?"

"Dad, except for a bad haircut and a sore spot on the top of my head, I'm mended. It's not as if I feel faint or anything. Besides, I did ask you to drive me. All I want to do is go in and speak to her for a few minutes. I'll hardly hurt myself doing that."

Avery shrugged, looked around to see if Martha was in the vicinity, and said to Lewis, "If we drift quietly into the garage, we might be able to drive there and back without getting in trouble."

Two minutes later, with Avery waiting in the car, Lewis knocked at Maple's door. Itsy Powers answered and scurried off to see if the hostess was receiving guests. She soon returned and ushered Lewis upstairs, and when he tapped at the bedroom door, a voice called, "*Entrez*, Lewis."

Lewis entered the room and smiled at Maple, and she smiled at him, and they both sort of laughed. "I'm glad to see you looking so well, Mrs. Baderhoovenlisterah."

"Hogwash, Lewis. I'm looking pale and worn out."

Although Maple did seem older than Lewis had ever seen her appear, he said, "You look fresh to me."

Maple smirked. "That bang on your head has obviously affected your vision, Lewis. How are you otherwise?"

"Fine. Just a little tender on top. I can't stay long. Dad's out front with the car running. I came to thank you for saving my life."

"Yes . . . well, maybe I did tide you over for a bit," Maple offered modestly, then added, "I was proud to do it, too, Lewis. Being associated with a daredevil like you is a real honor. Do tell, what's next on your adventurous agenda?"

"Going to France."

"Yes, I know."

"You know? Not to be rude, Mrs. Bader-hoovenlisterah, but how could you possibly know that?"

A shrewd little grin appeared on Maple's face. "I know because that adorable Amanda

Dot stopped by yesterday evening to see how I was doing. She stayed a spell, and we talked."

"Oh, I see." Lewis grew pensive. "I hope Amanda doesn't tell everyone. It'd be a disaster if Mom heard what I'm planning before I had a chance to speak with her."

Maple's shrewd grin grew shrewder. "Funny, I used practically the same words when I mentioned that possibility to Amanda. You have no cause for worry, Lewis. She understands and agreed to be discreet. Incidentally, she's a catch if I've ever seen one."

Lewis shuffled his feet and looked down, and in one of those phenomena that sometimes occur in nature, his cheeks turned the exact color of a Pompadour Rose.

TWENTY

That evening after supper the Hintons were enjoying the evening air on the back patio when they heard a knock at the front door. Avery got up to see who it was and soon returned with Turly Sweed and Tom Fitzboken. Tom was carrying Lewis's maroon beret. He bid his respects to Martha, and said to Lewis, "I brought this for you. It came floating downriver a short while before you did."

"Thank you, Mr. Fitzboken. It looks in pretty good shape."

"The missus ironed it for you. It got me to thinking of the blue beret I once had, so I ordered one from a catalog Mayor Greenly has in her store. She liked the idea and ordered a whole pile of berets. Only problem is, she special-ordered for words to be printed on them. I told her I wanted mine blank."

"What words did she order?" asked Lewis.

Tom smiled dubiously. "Can't say for sure.

She was still trying to decide when I left the store, but she was thinking along the lines of 'Slippery Falls: Home of Divine People.'"

"I can't believe I voted for that woman," Martha remarked with a snort, then said to Avery, "Come, honey. Let's go put some coffee on, and let these gentlemen speak with Lewis for a moment."

As his parents departed, Lewis placed his beret atop the bandage on his head and thanked the visitors for saving his life.

His gratitude was waved off by Turly, who said, "Enough of that. We've been thanked and honored too much as it is. We didn't do anything a decent person like you wouldn't have done if the situation were reversed."

"Speaking of decent," remarked Tom. "We've come to offer our apologies for mocking you the way we did. It wasn't proper to treat a fellow fisherman like that."

"And a remarkable fisherman he is," adjoined Turly.

Lewis was not only surprised by the men's respectful manner, he was confused. "Did something happen that I don't know about?"

Turly and Tom exchanged glances, then Tom said, "That's more or less what we wanted to ask you. That big trout you were after, how big is it?"

The vague hint of a memory stirred in Lewis, and he thought maybe he knew what was perplexing Turly and Tom. Lewis felt a laugh coming on and replied, "You probably wouldn't believe me if I told you how big."

"We might," suggested Turly.

"Well . . ." said Lewis. "It was about the size of a torpedo."

"You said was," Tom observed.

"Indeed, I did say was," Lewis replied. "That trout got away. I doubt if anyone could catch it now."

The two men exchanged glances again. Both paused to ponder individually, then Turly reached to shake Lewis's hand. "If you ever want to join us on the bridge, we'd be glad to have you."

"That goes for Hank and me, too," added Tom.

Lewis's laugh broke loose. "Thanks for the offer. I may just take you up on it one day."

Lewis was sunning on the back patio the next morning when he heard the muted sound of Amanda's voice. She was in the living room, chatting with Martha. Although Lewis could not discern what they were discussing, the back-and-forth rhythm of their speech suggested they were intimately engaged in conversation. Since when, he wondered, had Amanda and Martha become so close? An alarm clanged in his heart. There was danger in the making of that pair.

The next thing he knew they were in the kitchen, where he could clearly hear Martha say, "So dear, you're in charge while Avery and I go shopping. We shouldn't be more than an hour. If Lewis acts up, send him to his room."

"I'll do that, Martha," Amanda said with a giggle.

Lewis cringed. Amanda had used his mother's first name!

A dulcet voice returned him to the here and now. "Hello, Lewis. How are you feeling today?"

"Okay," Lewis muttered, acutely aware of a new element of shyness between Amanda and him. This mutual reticence, however, did not hamper her ability to direct a conversation, and she said, "Before I forget, Sophie said to tell you she's ready to resume French lessons whenever you feel up to the task."

"Thanks for the message," Lewis replied timidly. The less said about Sophie at the moment, the better for him.

Perhaps Amanda felt the same way, for she moved immediately to the next subject on her list. "What you said about going to France, is that a definite decision?"

"Maybe."

" 'Maybe' is not definite, Lewis."

"I mean, yes . . . if I can figure out a way to pay for it."

Amanda nodded. She'd already thought the matter through. "That's why I'm here. You know how I love helping people."

"I do, but how can you help me pay for a trip to France? I know you aren't rich."

"There're ways around that. The easiest route, I think, would be a charity car wash."

Lewis was skeptical. "And exactly what qualifies me as a charity?"

Amanda wriggled her nose and explained, "Obviously you'd be a cultural-exchange ambassador from Slippery Falls. Mayor Greenly will eat it up. Besides, we're teenagers. No one will question us holding a car wash."

Lewis was temporarily at a loss for words.

Not Amanda. "We'll go over the numbers another day, after you get better. In the meantime, leave the details to me. If we are going to hold a charitable event, we might as well make it a big one."

Lewis felt a novel emotion rise up in him. It was warm at the core and gleeful around the edges. "I must say, Amanda, you're an impressive thinker — not to mention a wonderful singer and a precious friend."

"Nice of you to say so."

"It's true."

Amanda twittered coquettishly. "Listen to you, Lewis. It almost sounds like you're flirting."

Lewis thought: *I am*. He said, "Anything's possible."

Amanda blushed a little and asked, "So, have you told your parents yet about going to France?"

"No." Lewis hesitated before adding, "Maybe I will tonight."

● ● ●

Lewis waited until the plates were cleared from the dinner table before presenting his idea to Martha and Avery. He started soft. "Mom. Dad. Just wondering, what would you think if I told you I sent away for my passport?"

Martha saw immediately where the question pointed. "I'd think you decided to go look for your natural mother. Have you?"

"No. Or yes. I mean, I'd like to visit France for a few weeks in August, if I can find the money."

Martha pursed her lips, then startled both Avery and Lewis by saying, "Going to France is not something teenagers from Idaho usually do, but then Lewis has never been usual. It sounds very exciting to me."

Lewis's jaw dropped. "It does?"

"It does," Martha told Lewis, then turned to Avery. "Don't you think so, dear?"

Avery went with the flow. "Exciting sounds right to me."

Then a funny, far-off look entered Martha's

eyes, and she observed, "Of course, to a small-town girl like me who hasn't seen the ocean since her honeymoon, going anywhere sounds exciting. Lewis, if you want to visit France, I won't stand in your way."

"Thank you, Mom. Thank you, thank you," Lewis gushed with heartfelt emotion.

Avery beamed happily and said to Martha, "You know, dear, if Lewis went away for a few weeks in August, you and I'd be free for a road trip to the Oregon coast. Might be fun to wriggle our toes in the ocean again."

"Ooh, Avery," Martha cooed. "That sounds Exciting with a capital E."

Five minutes later, Lewis was standing by the phone in the hallway, about to dial Amanda Dot's number, when Avery sauntered by and remarked, "Good old Martha. I doubt they make 'em that fine in France."

TWENTY-ONE

Lewis healed rapidly, and by the Saturday after his accident was ready to resume schooling in the French language. Sophie came to the house, and they studied on the back patio. Although Lewis was not what anyone would call a precocious student, Sophie was a patient instructor and together they made some progress. However, with Lewis hoping to depart for France in mid-August, Sophie felt the need to accelerate his learning curve. "If you're serious about this, Lewis, we have to step up your lessons to three a week, and you have to study on your own at least two hours a day."

"Think that'll make me fluent?"

"Not even close," Sophie replied with alacrity. "But perhaps you'll be able to buy a loaf of bread and find a bathroom."

"That'd help." Lewis grinned. "I don't

think I could hold it in the whole time I'm there."

Amanda came on Sunday to help Lewis determine his financial requirements for the trip. First she got on the phone and called all the listed 1-800 airline numbers. The least expensive round-trip between Idaho Falls, Idaho, and Paris, France, with a student discount, came to seven hundred and ten dollars, including tax. Afterward, assuming a two-week stay at a minimum of forty dollars a day for lodging, food, and gift buying, plus an additional two hundred dollars for travel to and from Versailles, Amanda derived a target sum of fourteen hundred and seventy dollars. "To be on the safe side, let's call it fifteen hundred."

Lewis stated that he had four hundred and ninety-one dollars in savings, and that Avery had offered to advance his allowance for one year, which added an additional five hundred and twenty.

Amanda added in her head. "That gives you one thousand and eleven dollars."

Lewis subtracted in his head. "Which leaves me four hundred and eighty-nine short."

"If we charge fifteen dollars a car and twenty dollars a truck, and we get forty dirty vehicles . . . not a problem. In fact, you should have money to spare."

"If that's what happens, Amanda, you should keep everything over four hundred and eighty-nine."

Amanda scoffed. "Don't be vulgar. I wouldn't take a dime. Of course . . ." Her frown lifted into a smile. "If you were walking around Paris and saw a silk scarf in a window, I wouldn't be offended if you remembered me."

Lewis chuckled. "How could I forget you?"

"It's unlikely, I know."

On Thursday, July the twelfth, Martha and Lewis went to Doc Riddle's to have the bandage and stitches removed from Lewis's head. After accomplishing these tasks and inspecting the healed wound, Doc told Lewis, "Except for where I cut away your hair, you look fine. Don't swim in dirty water or play any contact sports. Otherwise, go about your normal business."

"That's all the advice he gets?" Martha reproached Doc.

"I'm a medical practitioner, not a guidance counselor."

Although Martha's expression suggested Doc Riddle might be in for a stinging retort, she replied graciously, "And a very good one at that, Doc. Slippery Falls is lucky to have you."

Doc bowed. "I'm touched."

During the coming weeks, Lewis made limited progress with his French, visited his new fishermen friends on the bridge, spent lots of time with Amanda (although they operated under the umbrella of "just friends," they were sneaking up on becoming a couple), and went about his normal business as Doc had advised. Generally speaking, all went fairly well for Lewis, except for one thing: Maple. The remarkable old woman had bounced back physically after two weeks of bed rest, but now suffered from mild depression, or as she put it, "I've lost my plot."

In many ways, Lewis felt responsible for her inclement spirits. He was sitting in the park one day, listening to the waterfall when an inspired idea popped into his head. He got up and went straight to Maple's house.

"It's me again," he said when she greeted him at the door.

"What brings you?"

"I found your plot."

"Pardon me?"

"Your plot," Lewis repeated. "I figured out what you should do next."

Maple was either amused or annoyed. One could not say which from the look on her face. "Pray tell, what do you figure?"

"You should begin a campaign for the reopening of the Slippery Falls Public Library. You're a perfect spearhead for the effort and would make a great head librarian."

Maple's face furrowed in thought, and for a moment Lewis was afraid he had offended her. Then her left eyebrow arched up, and a wrinkle of interest appeared on her forehead. "Hmmm," she hemmed. "Sounds like something Madame de Pompadour might do."

"Definitely," seconded Lewis.

"Hmmm. Hmm. If I were head librarian, I'd dedicate a whole room just for epics."

"Brilliant idea," Lewis cheered.

Maple shot a warning look at Lewis. "Don't rush me, young man. I haven't decided anything yet."

"Of course not."

"I need to mull it over for awhile."

"Of course you do."

● ● ●

Lewis's passport arrived on July twenty-third. The next day Amanda reserved him a flight to Paris for the twelfth of August.

The car wash was on Saturday, August fourth. It was held on Main Street, beside Slippery Falls Park, with water from a hydrant Mayor Greenly gave them permission to use. She documented the whole affair with a video camera. Somewhere in the back of her mind was a notion that 60 Minutes might air the tape.

A table was set up on the sidewalk. Amanda handled the money while the vehicles were hand-washed by Gaston, Misty, Lewis, Lob, Sophie, and a bunch of volunteers from Slippery Falls High. The scrubbers took turns operating the hose. Something about that flexible tube invited monkey business and gave Misty cause to quip, "We should've charged extra for showers."

The gang worked from nine A.M. until half past three in the afternoon. When they were done, there were forty-four somewhat cleaner vehicles in Slippery Falls: twenty-three cars, sixteen pickup trucks, three forklifts that Morton Fullup personally drove down from the ladder factory, and two garden wagons that Itsy Powers and Maple Baderhoovenlisterah pulled to the park and insisted on having washed at full pickup truck price.

The take for the day was seven hundred and sixty-five dollars, well over Lewis's financial needs.

The following week passed in a blur of preparations and heady conversations for Lewis. What a difference three months had made in his story. In May he was a veritably dysfunctional soul who didn't know who he was or have much hope of finding out, and now . . . well, now he was a satisfied fisherman named Lewis "Poisson" Hinton, on the brink of flying to Europe. It was beyond his storytelling scope to have ever imagined this narrative.

He bolted up in bed in the middle of the night before the day of his departure. He could hardly believe Martha had endorsed the idea of his trip. Her only articulated worry was that Lewis would get lonely in a place where no one knew his name. It was not an apprehension he shared, for he'd recently concluded that people who know themselves never truly get lonely.

Somehow, Lewis fell back asleep and did not awake until morning. He went through the motions of getting dressed and eating breakfast, yet had a strange feeling that he was still dreaming last night's dreams. The feeling lasted until the moment he picked up his traveling bags and followed his parents out of the house.

They were met by loud cheering and were immediately engulfed in a throng of well-wishers. Lewis found himself face-to-face with Maple. "*Bon voyage*," she chirped, opening a kerchief over Lewis's head and sprinkling him with rose petals. "You'll have a job waiting when you get back."

"What kind of job?"

"Shelving books, sweeping floors, and doing whatever the library director tells you to do."

"That's excellent, Mrs. Baderhoovenlisterah. I almost can't wait to go and come back."

Gaston stepped forward and embraced Lewis warmly. "Hang in there, man, and don't take any crap from those cheese lovers."

Then Sophie sidled forth and pecked Lewis's cheek. "I wish you a king's fortune."

Sophie withdrew, and it was Amanda's turn to say good-bye. "I have something for you to remember me by."

"You do?" said Lewis.

Amanda nodded, placed both of her hands behind Lewis's head, pulled his face to hers, and kissed him squarely and at length on the lips. Whether it was a French kiss or an American smooch is none of the reader's beeswax. The exchange exhilarated Amanda and ensured that Lewis would not be forgetting her for a long, long time to come.

Lewis had put his bags in the trunk of the car and was waving in general to the crowd when Lob Borroughs shouted, "Hey Lewis, they speak French in France. How are you going to communicate?"

"I've been studying French."

"Yeah, right," said Lob. "Let's hear some."

"Go ahead, Lewis," chimed Misty. "Give us a line."

Lewis waited for silence before saying, *"Bonjour. Je m'appelle Louis. Je suis venu apprendre la langue et la tradition de mes ancêtres. Pouvez-vous m'amener à Versailles?"* Then he got in the car, and Avery backed out of the driveway.

Those remaining turned to Sophie, who gladly obliged with a translation. "He said, 'Hello. My name is Louis. I have come to learn the language and ways of my people. Can you deliver me to Versailles?' "